CW00349122

THE MATCHMAKER, THE APPRENTICE, AND THE FOOTBALL FAN

WEATHERHEAD BOOKS ON ASIA

WEATHERHEAD EAST ASIAN INSTITUTE

COLUMBIA UNIVERSITY

THE
THE
AND THE

TRANSLATED BY JULIA LOVELL

MATCHMAKER, APPRENTICE, FOOTBALL FAN

MORE STORIES OF CHINA

COLUMBIA UNIVERSITY PRESS   NEW YORK

COLUMBIA UNIVERSITY PRESS
Publishers Since 1893
New York Chichester, West Sussex
cup.columbia.edu

This book brings together the following short stories, first published in Chinese as:
"Chi le yi ge cangying" (The Matchmaker), 1993
"Dama de yuqi" (Dama's Way of Talking), 1995
"Zuikui huoshou shi Manaduola" (The Football Fan), 1997
"Yi ge shixisheng" (The Apprentice), 1998
"Zai Jiaoyu" (Reeducation), 1998
"Kan nüren" (Xiao Liu), 1999
"Hu Laoshi, jintian xiawu qu da lanqiu ma?" (Mr. Hu, Are You Coming Out to Play Basketball This Afternoon?), 1999
"Paizhen matou" (The Wharf), 2009

This publication has been supported by the Richard W. Weatherhead Publication Fund of the East Asian Institute, Columbia University.

Library of Congress Cataloging-in-Publication Data

Zhu, Wen, 1967–
[Works. Selections]
The Matchmaker, the Apprentice, and the Football Fan : More Stories of China / Zhu Wen ; translated by Julia Lovell.
pages cm. — (Weatherhead Books on Asia)
ISBN 978-0-231-16090-2 (cloth : alk. paper) — ISBN 978-0-231-53507-6 (e-book)
1. China—Fiction. I. Lovell, Julia, 1975– II. Title.

PL2852.W424A2 2013
895.1'352—dc23

2012043112

Columbia University Press books are printed on permanent and durable acid-free paper.
This book is printed on paper with recycled content.
Printed in the United States of America

C 10 9 8 7 6 5 4 3 2 1

COVER & BOOK DESIGN BY VIN DANG | COVER ART BY ISTOCKPHOTO

CONTENTS

A NOTE ABOUT CHINESE NAMES AND ROMANIZATION *VII*
ACKNOWLEDGMENTS *IX*

DA MA'S **WAY OF TALKING** *1*
THE **MATCHMAKER** *19*
THE **APPRENTICE** *48*
THE **FOOTBALL FAN** *63*
XIAO **LIU** *77*
MR. HU, ARE YOU COMING OUT TO PLAY BASKETBALL THIS AFTERNOON? *107*
REEDUCATION *124*
THE **WHARF** *147*

A NOTE ABOUT CHINESE NAMES AND ROMANIZATION

In Chinese names, the surname is given first, followed by the given name. Therefore, in the case of Liu Guixiang, Liu is the surname and Guixiang is the given name.

In the pinyin system of romanization, transliterated Chinese is pronounced as in English, apart from the following sounds:

VOWELS

A	(when it is the only letter following most single consonants, except for t): *a,* as in after
AI	*eye*
AO	*ow,* as in cow
E	*uh*
EI	*ay,* as in may
EN	*en,* as in happen
ENG	*ung,* as in lung
I	(when it is the only letter following most consonants): *e,* as in she
I	(when following c, ch, s, sh, zh, z): *er,* as in writer
IA	*yah*
IAN	*yen*
IE	*yeah*

IU	*yo,* as in yo-yo
O	*o,* as in stork
ONG	*oong*
OU	*o,* as in so
U	(when following most consonants): *oo,* as in loot
U	(when following j, q, x, y): *ü,* like the German ü
UA	*wah*
UAI	*why*
UAN	*wu-an*
UANG	*wu-ang*
UI	*way*
UO	*u-woah*
YAN	*yen*
YI	*ee,* as in feed

CONSONANTS

C	*ts,* as in bits
Q	a slightly more sibilant version of *ch,* as in choose
X	a slightly more sibilant version of *sh,* as in sheep
Z	*ds,* as in woods
ZH	*j,* as in jump

ACKNOWLEDGMENTS

Early drafts of "Da Ma's Way of Talking" and "The Wharf" appeared, respectively, in *Words Without Borders* and *Odyssey: Architecture and Literature*. The translation of "Xiao Liu" was first commissioned and published (as "How to Look at Women") by Comma Press (www.commapress.co.uk) for the anthology *Shi Cheng: Short Stories from Urban China* (2012), edited by Liu Ding, Carol Yinghua Lu, and Ra Page, with support of the Confucius Institute at the University of Manchester. I am grateful to these publications for permission to reproduce this material here.

THE MATCHMAKER, THE APPRENTICE, AND THE FOOTBALL FAN

DA MA'S WAY OF TALKING

THE MATCHMAKER
THE APPRENTICE
THE FOOTBALL FA
XIAO LIU
MR. HU, ARE YOU COM
REEDUCATIO
THE WHARF

In the summer of 1989, I was assigned to a job in an electrical engineering company in Nanjing. My train pulled in at one in the afternoon, and as I walked out of the station—two large bags slung over my shoulder—I was ambushed by a mob of peasant girls delegated by hotels to pester people for business. The sweat was pouring off me, and I was not in a good mood. "Get lost," I told them. "I live here; I don't need a hotel."

The clueless cousin of mine who'd said he'd meet me off the train hadn't showed up. (I'd told him to not to, but he'd insisted.) So I decided my best option was to look for a shady place to get a cold drink down me while I waited. The Nanjing summer has a talent for making you feel like an internal organ—hot, sticky, visceral, the blood pulsing through you—trapped inside the crowded, overheated body of the city.

The moment I sat down by a phone box, I was set upon yet again, this time by a number of vexingly self-confident females soliciting for another kind of custom. Who the hell thinks about sex when they're getting roasted alive? Maybe you do, but I felt sick at the idea of it. After expressing their very poor opinion of me and salting their assessment with a few bonus obscenities, they and their substantial buttocks sashayed off in the direction of another unfortunate. Just as my ears were joyfully anticipating a moment of peace, they tuned into a voice coming from inside the phone booth behind me.

The delivery was fast, relentless, intensely rhythmical, and the two most frequently recurring phrases were "Great fuck!" and "You're fucking dead!" And the laugh: an aural whiplash, far outside the repertoire of sounds associated with conventional human voice production. The voice warmed me, anchored me, convinced me I'd chanced on an old friend in a strange town. But when I turned to identify the speaker, I discovered I'd never met him before in my life.

He stood—tall, burly—one hand propped against the wall of the booth, the words charging out of him. I stared at him through the dark brown glass. I couldn't help myself: the longer I listened to him, the harder it was for me to accept that I didn't actually know him. Soon enough, he noticed me, too, and glared menacingly back. I went on staring, obliviously. After a little while, he hung up, stormed out of the booth, and pushed me, hard, in the chest. I noted a coiled snake tattooed on his right arm. He was, I realized as he walked up to me, a serious physical presence. It crossed my mind that I might have found myself some trouble.

"What the hell were you looking at me like that for?" I no longer recognized his voice; it was completely different from the one he'd used a few seconds ago on the phone—he instantly seemed to me like another person.

"I was just thinking that we might have a friend in common."

"You and me?"

"Do you by any chance know Da Ma?"

"Are you a friend of his?"

“Yes, we were at college together in Beijing. I thought you—”

“Hmm. Well. Forget it then. Not out of love for that bastard Da Ma, though.”

He pulled a cigarette out of my shirt pocket, lit up, then walked around me and off in the direction of the number 1 bus stop.

“D’you know where he lives?” I shouted after him.

“I’d like to know myself where the lying bastard is. He’ll be a dead man when I find him.”

All this happened on my first day in Nanjing. I’ve since wasted a good five years of my life here, but not once has my path crossed Da Ma’s. Of course, neither have I particularly sought him out; he wasn’t that good a friend. For me, like for a lot of my classmates, he was the sort of friend you’d be happy to bump into by chance, but not the sort you’d make a special effort to look up. He was as he talked: edgy, restless, furiously impatient. So I suspected he’d already left Nanjing some way behind him. But I was sure that he’d stayed here a while, that he’d left his mark on the place.

Of the friends that I was to make in the city, three had met Da Ma. I spotted them and the unmistakable style of delivery they’d picked up from him, instantly. None had particularly warm feelings toward him—they all had, it appeared, suffered at his hands—and none knew his current whereabouts. But listening to them was like listening to Da Ma himself, like being back in his company.

Da Ma’s style of talking—exhilarating, bewildering, overwhelming—was, it is no exaggeration to say, like an acutely infectious disease or a communicable fungus; and once it had gotten you, trouble never seemed to be far away. But there was a beautiful lexical economy to it. To anything or anyone that pissed you off, the only appropriate response was, “You’re fucking dead!” For happenings at the other end of the gratification spectrum, “Great fuck!” enjoyed an equally broad application. I can still remember Da Ma’s favorite rhythm of speech, and it went something like this:

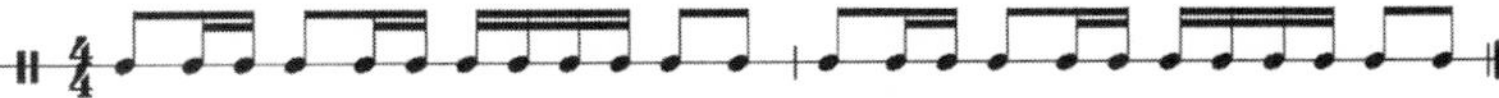

(For added authenticity, accompany with vigorous agitation of the arms, à la Da Ma.)

My second day at college, our whole class was sent to northeast China for a month's training in a People's Liberation Army barracks. Freshmen these days are a bit more delicate than we were, a bit more flaky, so they get sent for three months—a supremely expeditious means of improving organization and discipline in the new cohort. From day 1, I yearned only for our final test: the shooting range. At school, I'd been a crack shot with an air gun—and a bad place for small, inoffensive birds to find themselves around—and I was desperate to show off to my new classmates.

Eventually, my moment of glory drew near. Identically rigged up in our army uniforms, we sat in formation on the drill ground, awaiting orders under an angry sun. When your name was called by the duty captain, you stood up, formed an orderly line, and then proceeded into the shooting range—ten at a time because there were only ten targets. I soon picked up on a student in the row in front of me: short, skinny, more fretfully impatient than even I was, rattling away indiscriminately to the people on either side of him, neither of whom seemed particularly interested in taking any notice. After the first round of gunshots rang out, he yelped and leaped up.

"They've fired!" he shouted hysterically around at us. "They've finally fired!"

Laughter scattered across the drill ground. He then made as if to charge off in the direction of the shooting range but was captured and pushed back in line by the sunburned soldier in charge of maintaining discipline. He reluctantly sat back down, muttering away to himself and eliciting further laughter from his audience. A number of his comrades in arms tried to provoke more of a performance out of him, but he ignored them, falling sulkily silent. This unremarkable-looking, slightly undersized individual, I may as well reveal now, was Da Ma.

Our department, I remember, had drawn the short straw that day; we'd been scheduled to shoot last of all, after every other class had finished. After two scorching hours serenaded by other people's gunfire, we were just about catatonic. I'd have left if they'd let me. Of course, though, when the captain called my name, I perked up again fast enough. Da Ma was number 4 in my group; I was number 7. The captain took up position behind the student in front of the first target and barked: Lie down! We all complied. My hands were trembling as they loaded the gun (from excitement, naturally). When everyone had taken aim, we waited for the captain to give the order to fire. I took several deep breaths, savoring the acrid scent of burned gunpowder hanging over the range.

It was at this instant that Da Ma, at target number 4, sprang up and pointed his semiautomatic rifle at the people to his left.

"Freeze! Or you're fucking dead!"

Screaming, the girls in front of targets 1 and 2 curled up into balls on the ground, covering their heads with their arms. "Fucking hell!" the boy at number 3 began gibbering, "That gun's loaded! Fuck, fuck, fucking fuck!"

"I know," Da Ma replied. "That's why I told you to freeze. Hands behind your head!"

The captain, still in front of target number 1, turned an interesting shade of white. "Stop screwing around, you little bastard," he snarled, then began to approach Da Ma.

Da Ma swung the gun directly at him.

"Freeze!" he shouted again. "That goes for you, too! Stay where you are!"

The captain stopped in his tracks. To my eternal regret, my prostrate position meant I was unable to see for myself the expression on Da Ma's face; it was something I could only guess at by contemplating the ghastly pallor with which the captain's face had responded. The two of them squared off at each other—for how long I can't remember, but what seemed like a good long time. Suddenly, we heard laughter, Da Ma's laughter, gusting over the drill ground. Considering his joke to have drawn to a tidy, natural close, Da Ma placed his gun on the ground and then lay back down, as if readying himself to shoot. The captain immediately charged over, grabbed hold of the back of Da Ma's collar, yanked him to his feet, then pushed him out of the shooting range. "What the hell," I remember a bewildered Da Ma protesting, "what the hell . . ."

When we returned to campus at the end of that month, Da Ma was briskly and severely punished by the university administration, although according to our teacher, the authorities had been remarkably lenient. I don't know whether Da Ma truly was as unbothered as he acted. At any rate, on he went, exactly as before, scuttling from one dormitory to another, rattling unstoppably away at anyone he found there.

Within a term, everyone who roomed with him talked like him, principally to complain about him. Within a year, I think that everyone in our department had at least a touch of Da Ma in the way they talked; it was an unavoidable, incurable condition. Da Ma struck me as someone permanently on the edge, his tiny hands always flailing about as if desperately trying to grasp hold of something. But what?

In truth, if I'd been forced to spend every day in his company, I wouldn't have been able to put up with him any better than his roommates could. Da Ma had a trick of rubbing things in when you were unhappy; his exuberance seemed to feed off your own troubles. There was something about him that never quite meshed with the rest of us, that made us wary. And so he took to spending more and more time off campus, getting mixed up with dubious characters and dubious outcomes. How did Da Ma get that new cut on his head?, we'd often be asking ourselves. Where did he get that designer jacket?

One Saturday afternoon, in the first semester of our third year, he tiptoed across one of our dormitories and gave a significant push to a classmate on window-cleaning duty. Fortunately, as he was only three floors up, the ejectee wound up breaking nothing more serious than a leg. Da Ma vigorously defended himself as ever, in distinctive Da Ma tones: It'd been a joke, he protested, how was he to know his victim hadn't been holding on properly? I believed him—that it really had been a joke—but this time, Da Ma had gone too far.

When the moment came for Da Ma to pack up his things and go home for the last time, our teacher tried—in rhetorical rhythms learned from Da Ma himself—to console him, to get him to see the bright side. "Great fuck!" Da Ma responded cheerfully enough, then got up to leave. But when he reached the dormitory door, he burst into tears, sat himself down on the floor, and refused to get up. "You don't have to leave today," the teacher backtracked. "You can stay on a bit longer. But sooner or later, you'll have to go." We watched and listened as Da Ma's sobs grew louder, more heartbroken. After he finally returned home for good, we often thought of him—on account of his still owing us money or meal tickets.

✶

My second year in Nanjing, I met my girlfriend, Xiao Chu. One summer's day, at a Chinese fast-food place, I heard a girl on the table next to me talking very emphatically to her escort—a quiet, docile-looking young man who had politely set down his chopsticks to dedicate himself to listening. I walked over and told her I needed to ask her something. Although this overture would eventually lead me to become Xiao Chu's boyfriend, at that moment in time that enviable position was filled by her current dining companion. It was Da Ma who lobbed this particular ball of destiny into my lap, knocking me off balance into the quicksand of romance. Thanks, Da Ma—I think.

"Do you know someone called Da Ma?"

"Doma? Who the hell's he?"

"No, Da Ma. Da—Ma: D—A—M—A."

"You fascinate me. You *are* fascinating. But I don't know a Ma Da."

"It's Da Ma."

"I don't know a Da Ma either. Anything else you wanted to get off your chest?"

And that—that was how it all began between us. For ages, Xiao Chu refused to believe that Da Ma genuinely existed. She thought it was one of my standard pickup lines, that I was in the habit of walking up to pretty girls and asking them if they knew Da Ma. But my faith in my own judgment was not so easily shaken, and I conducted a careful investigation of her colleagues at the advertising agency where she worked, of her relatives and former boyfriends. Not a whiff of Da Ma.

"Xiao Chu, did you always used to talk like that?"

"How should I know?"

"Listen to me, you must have met Da Ma at some point. Maybe you didn't know that was his name."

"OK, here's the deal. If you shut up about Da Ma *right now,* you can see me again."

"I'm not joking, you must have—"

"One more Da Ma, and you're fucking dead!"

I was determined to trace out the path of infection. Pointless obstinacy on my part? If you'd heard Da Ma and heard Xiao Chu, you'd have seen, or heard, what I meant. Just as I hit a cul-de-sac in my investigations, something most unexpected occurred. I suddenly realized that I had fallen in love with their temperamental subject. While, of course, this inevitably gave me more opportunities to search for clues, it also rather distracted me from the job at hand. For the time being, the whole Da Ma puzzle had to be set to one side. Having said that, though, it was impossible to shut him completely out of my mind because it was only through my fights with Xiao Chu that our relationship began to get somewhere.

The pattern went something like this: there'd be a minor quarrel every day, a major one every three. Now, when it comes to arguments, I'm no pushover—I'd probably get the better of you—but Xiao Chu was in a league of her own. Once she hit her stride, it was like she was possessed: if I closed my eyes, there Da Ma was, in the room with me again, flinging his hands about like a lunatic. Arguing with him, or her, was like playing squash against yourself: the harder you hit the ball, the faster, the more deviously it came back at you. Exhausted by each defeat, I felt only tender humility before my all-conquering antagonist, and it was in the calms that followed the storms of our fights that our feelings for each other deepened.

As soon as we'd finished a big argument, Xiao Chu would tidy her hair and then drag me out to the eastern suburbs of Nanjing to take photos of her. I've never known anyone with such a passion for being photographed. She'd had three boyfriends (not including me; the current incumbent didn't usually feature in her statistics), and each had left her with (at least) one souvenir photo album, all specializing in one subject. As number 4, I enjoyed the great good fortune of being able to study at my leisure the subtle differences and variations in my predecessors' aesthetic perspectives on, and understanding of, Xiao

Chu. I felt, I must say, that making an original contribution to this already well-populated, exhaustively documented field of endeavor represented a significant, perhaps an insurmountable, challenge.

Xiao Chu's best and oldest friend, Lian Xiang, worked in the coloring and enlarging department of a mimeographing service. For years now, she had been logistically facilitating Xiao Chu's photographic mania. I had no great love of Lian Xiang, of her delicately drawn face dulled by melancholy. She was always bringing out the worst in Xiao Chu. This Lian Xiang, I might as well tell you, had from day 1 gone out of her way to make life difficult for me. In all the time that I've been seeing Xiao Chu, not once has Lian Xiang given me an opportunity to get to know her properly. She once told me that she'd done self-defense. Why should I have believed her? With the benefit of hindsight, though, take it from me—I should have believed her.

But the worst of the whole business was that almost every day, Xiao Chu and Lian Xiang would curl up in bed together, debating and discussing anything—everything that came into their heads. There seemed to be no limit to the things they had to say to each other. And sometimes, inevitably, they got onto the subject of me. Don't think I underestimated Lian Xiang intellectually—far from it. I'm sure she spent most of her time advising Xiao Chu on the most treacherous techniques for keeping me under control. All this, of course, was conjecture on my part. Maybe I should have hired someone to kidnap her and sell her off in some remote rural area, to clear the field for me with Xiao Chu. Would this have been a solution, I wonder? It was, in any case, an idea I got from Lian Xiang in the first place, via Xiao Chu. At any rate, this Lian Xiang was one mighty pain in the neck. Now *she* was someone I wanted to say "You're Fucking Dead!" to.

Where was I? My relationship with Xiao Chu is another story altogether. A writer, gentle reader, is an individual of iron self-control. If I seem rather to have lost it here, it is entirely because of the mischief of one Da Ma.

*

Sometimes I felt sorry for Da Ma, watching him wandering in and out of our department's dormitories like a stray dog, ignored by everyone. So one day in the washroom, I flashed him a friendly smile. He made straight for me. Events, I immediately realized, might have taken a turn not necessarily harmonious with my own best interests.

"Would you consider yourself a friend of mine?" he asked me, very solemnly.

"Up until now—yes."

"And after that?"

"After that—I don't know." By which I meant that if he let me get on with washing this pile of clothes that had been moldering in a bucket for six long weeks now, I'd be willing to give the question serious thought.

Da Ma nodded, closed his eyes, breathed deeply a few times, then suddenly opened them again, wide.

"I have to tell you something. I have to tell someone—today. If I don't tell you, I'll tell someone else. But it might as well be you. Last night, I slept with Li Yuyu."

"With who?"

"You heard me."

"What I mean is, why the hell would she . . ." Li Yuyu was our English teacher, a recent graduate of Beijing Foreign Languages College, tall, well built, strong on self-esteem. She admitted very few Chinese into her circle of male acquaintances. By contrast, Da Ma was short, skinny—undersized in probably all respects.

"I know what you're thinking. So did she—to begin with. So that's what I made my main line of attack. I talked at her all night. Standing up, of course. In her room. I knew I'd break her. About five in the morning, just as it was starting to get light, she yawned and said to me, "'All right, you win, get into bed.' Ker-ching."

Before I'd recovered any useful degree of facial composure, Da Ma erupted into great raucous gasps of laughter, then executed a technically perfect about-turn, the kind of move he'd learned during military training.

“All right, I’m done. Get on with your washing.”

Listen to me, listen: I never believed him, not from the very start. Really. Was I jealous? I don’t know. At any rate, all that term, Da Ma was certainly full of the joys of spring. And whenever English class came round, he diligently caught up on his beauty sleep in the dormitory. Nor did he hand in any work. The fruits of his labors? A round two credits for English. But when something as extraordinary as that happened to Da Ma, no one gave it much thought because there were always far more perplexingly extraordinary things to get your head around. There were only two words to describe the whole curious business: Great Fuck!

While I was at college towards the end of the 1980s, debating was just starting to take off as an extracurricular activity in Chinese universities—there seemed, at that time, to be a lot more things worth arguing about than there had been in the past. Since the competition rules were not as perfectly regulated as they are now, I quietly suggested to our teacher that Da Ma represent our department in the specified-subject debating contest organized by the college chapter of the Communist Youth League. He had, you could say, a popular mandate to be chosen. Far from declining the honor, Da Ma used it, I heard, as an excuse to borrow ten *yuan* worth of meal tickets from the teacher in question.

As soon as we learned that his first-round opponent was the Department of Marxist-Leninist Thought, we knew things were going to get messy out there. Just before the debate, I eyed Da Ma on the right-hand side of the speakers’ platform, unlocking his shoulders, shrinking back into his seat, looking rather ill at ease in his new environment, while preparatory chaos—endless tugging on wires, setting up of microphones, and so on—reigned in the hall around him. By the time the umpire formally opened the debate, Da Ma was fast asleep. Waking with a start to an insistent poke on the shoulder, he slowly hauled himself to his feet, looking more than a touch disoriented. An unforgettable night began. There he stood through practically the whole debate, his flow of words staunched only, and very occasionally, by repeated high-volume interventions on the part of the umpire. Within minutes of beginning, he had succeeded in enraging everyone present—his opponent, the audience, even our department. Within another few minutes, the entire room was on fire.

It was not until proceedings were far advanced that the umpire realized that the passionate, if rather unstructured, debate had only one point in common with the contest's prescribed topic: both were in Chinese. Wiping the sweat off his forehead, he got up and wound his way around the referee's table and over to Da Ma. Comrade! he tried; no response. He then tapped Da Ma on the shoulder; no response. He tapped him again. Da Ma spun furiously around: "You're fucking dead!"

Our department, I hardly need say perhaps, lost the debate. It was too much to expect Da Ma to play by other people's rules. We shouldn't have done it to him. At the end of the contest, his face running with sweat, Da Ma stared down at the floor, too ashamed to look anyone in the eye. Little did he realize that he was by now a campus celebrity.

This seems as good a moment as any to annotate another of Da Ma's favorite rhythms:

After this heroic exposition in 4–4 time, Da Ma would sometimes surprise us all with a skittering development in 12–8 time:

Alternatively, if he happened to be in a good mood or if his audience were female, he would throw a touch of syncopation into the mix:

This is how he begged our head of department not to expel him:

Now this one, let me tell you, was no picnic to get the hang of, gasping the semiquaver rest at the start of each of the first four beats. Try it yourself and see what I mean.

Could I be missing Da Ma—just a little?

*

I began to notice, to my distress, that Xiao Chu was growing more extreme in her behavior. One day, in a clothes shop, she decided she wanted to try on a red T-shirt on display. So I looked around for the changing room. When I turned back, I discovered she'd already pulled off the top she'd come in, in front of everyone in the shop, then—with no sense of urgency or self-consciousness—was putting the red one on instead, surrounded by an embarrassed audience of innocent bystanders, of whom I was surely the most embarrassed.

On April 1, one easy phone call from her comfortable office left me kicking my heels uselessly at a local beauty spot for an entire afternoon. Just once a year—that I could have handled. But Xiao Chu decided to let me savor the rich hilarity of being an April fool as many times, and in as many ways, as it popped into her head. Quickly enough, I got wise to her and began trying to second-guess whether this or that assignation was a fool's errand. I always got it wrong. Then there'd be a scene—crying, screaming, the works. I would be reminded, repeatedly, that she hated people who didn't show up on time. Xiao Chu, I'm sure you'll have realized, was becoming a real cause for worry. What was the source of the problem?

"Listen to me, Xiao Chu. I'm begging you now; you have to change the way you talk."

"What way?" She was rocking back and forward on her chair.

"The way you talked just then. The way Da Ma talks."

"Here we go again. Who the hell is this Da Ma? Male, female? Animal, vegetable, mineral?"

"He used to be male, but I'm starting to wonder if he's had a sex change."

To prove how serious I was about the whole business, that day I ransacked all my cupboards, cases, and boxes in search of a picture of Da

Ma. All I could find was a group shot of four of us, taken in our first year at college in front of the summer palace at Chengde. Da Ma's hair was wild, his eyes glassy as they gazed off into the middle distance. An enormous, baggy white waistcoat flapped excessively about him; he was, in short, a vision of loveliness. The young man with a crew cut to the right of the group, bursting with youth, vitality, the promise of great things—that was me.

"Look at you! Great fuck. You look like you just rolled in from the paddy fields."

"It's him you're meant to be looking at! Him! That's Da Ma!"

"You could have pointed at any of them and said he was Da Ma, for all I care."

"No, look again. *That's* Da Ma. There's no one else like him."

"I'll give him this, he looks a damn sight more interesting than you."

"Thanks for that. Thanks a lot. If he walked in right now, then, I guess you'd jump him the moment he opened his mouth."

There was a brief, terrifying silence while Xiao Chu stared at the ground. She then flung her head back and screamed "Bastard!" at me, two tears trickling down her cheeks. I didn't have a chance after that, not after the tears.

One outcome of that day's argument was the violent bisection of my precious piece of photographic evidence. As luck would have it, though, both Da Ma and I escaped entirely unscarred. When I had a moment to subject Xiao Chu's behavior to a reasoned analysis, I concluded that her response indicated she was not yet an entirely lost cause. There was still the possibility of measure and control to her anger. After all, when directing her fury at the photograph, she'd lashed out—whether accidentally or on purpose—not at me but at a thoroughly unexceptional classmate of mine I couldn't have cared less about. I've always been an optimist.

From then on, whenever Xiao Chu and I were together, I would deliberately try to keep conversation to a bare minimum, to replace speech with gestures wherever I could. This was the first and most fundamental plank of my new strategy: to give Xiao Chu as little opportunity to speak as possible.

But one thing Xiao Chu was not short of was people to talk to; she always had a captive audience in Lian Xiang. And so I decided to seek out Lian Xiang to warn her of the likely consequences. This, it should be plain, was the action of a desperate man. One weekend, I invited the two of them over to my place for dinner. I'm sure you can understand what a painful sacrifice this represented for me.

Lian Xiang, by this point, I'd met a few times, without her making any kind of meaningful impression on me. This time was different, though. That evening, I caught the quality of intense quiet that muffled everything she did. She spoke so softly you'd miss it if you weren't listening; she padded along as silently as a cat—suddenly you'd turn and find her there, standing next to you. You know, I was starting to feel I wouldn't have minded a girlfriend like that. I was warming up to pointing this out to Xiao Chu. Maybe it would force her to take a long, hard look at herself. Maybe it wouldn't. It was, in any case, a plan B.

When Xiao Chu was in the kitchen, I grabbed the opportunity to explain my concerns to Lian Xiang. Xiao Chu must have caught something of it, because she began yelling from the other room: "Stop talking about me! Or you're fucking dead!"

But I had to tell Lian Xiang—whatever the consequences. I poured out the whole thing to her as concisely as I could and then waited for a response. She managed a faint smile; it didn't bring much light to the rest of her face.

"You really think there's something special about the way this Da Ma talks?"

Yes, yes, I repeated. But still I lacked proof—hard, conclusive proof. In the end, I resorted to digging out that old photo again. A cloud of melancholy passed slowly across her eyes.

"What did you just say he was called?"

"Da Ma."

"That's Da Ma?"

"That's Da Ma."

*

A week later, Xiao Chu called on me. She looked exhausted—all her usual, restless aggression seemed to have left her. The moment she walked in, she asked me for a cigarette, then lay back on the sofa, completely absorbed by the act of smoking. I watched, nonplussed by her new, weary serenity. I liked watching her smoke, I liked observing the intense concentration she brought to it—I could almost taste the pleasure of it myself. Her first cigarette finished, Xiao Chu drew another out of the pack and then finally began to speak.

"So you were telling the truth, after all."

"What d'you mean?"

"About Da Ma. He really does exist."

"Of course. You should have believed me in the first place."

Xiao Chu lit her second cigarette. Tantalized by the smell of tobacco, I lit one too. In the calm, deliberate tones in which she was speaking today, I glimpsed a gentleness I'd never noticed before.

"Lian Xiang's met Da Ma—did you know?"

"Has she?"

"More than met. She spent a night with him. Just one."

"Did she tell you that?"

"Yes. But he didn't tell her his real name. He called himself Li Jin. The address and phone number he gave her were false, too. So when she tried to get in touch with him, she got nowhere, of course. That was a year ago. Where d'you think the bastard is now?"

"How should I know? Somewhere."

"Maybe he's dead."

"Who knows. Does it matter?"

"I hope he's dead."

While I digested all this, Xiao Chu stubbed out her cigarette. I wanted to find out more, but her silence gave me pause.

When Xiao Chu looked back across at me, her eyes were shining with tears. "How could Lian Xiang have got so hung up on someone like that? I can't get my head round it. That Da Ma, he doesn't deserve her."

Though I had half a mind to argue, I kept it to myself. It would have been asking for trouble. But at least I was a step closer to solving one of my problems. I had finally got to the bottom of why Xiao Chu talked as she did. In that one night of passion, Da Ma had somehow, mysteriously, got under Lian Xiang's skin and then even more mysteriously had made his way under Xiao Chu's—that much I knew. And that is all I can tell you about this episode from a past life of mine.

*

In the autumn of 1993, on the highway that enters Tibet from Sichuan, Da Ma was stabbed through the liver and died instantly. This I learned from an electrical engineer called Chen Ran who, the summer before, had set off with my old classmate on foot from Xi'an, in the northwest. They'd had no particular destination in mind; they'd planned to travel only as far as their money lasted. As far as they could. "Halfway through, Da Ma told me he might not go any farther than Tibet." At this point, sitting opposite me, Chen Ran paused and sank deep into recollection. He seemed to age with every second that he spent in its company.

About half an hour later, his spirits appeared to recover a little. "In truth, though, Da Ma brought it on himself."

It had been evening, still very light, but the highway was completely deserted. After clambering up a slope, they saw a man heading down the other side. Chen Ran suggested they take a rest, and Da Ma agreed. But after he'd put down his bag, Da Ma suddenly set off in rapid pursuit of the man in front. Soon, he was at his heels. Chen Ran watched as he pulled out his dagger and shouted:

"Give us your money! Or you're fucking dead!"

This was probably the third time on the journey that Da Ma had tried cracking this particular joke—one of his favorites. But also, it turned out, his last. Slowly, the man turned around. Before Chen Ran had gotten a good look at his face, Da Ma's dagger was lodged below his own ribs.

Now I come to think of it, I probably should have written a more careful, a more profound piece about my friend Da Ma. But I know the attempt would have been doomed. Because in truth, I didn't really understand him. No one who'd spent any kind of time with Da Ma had managed to figure him out. But everyone remembered how he talked: thin lips slightly parted over blackened teeth, the syllables desperately forcing their way out: You're fucking dead.

Here, as a final appendix, is that ancient, vandalized photo of Da Ma, through which I hope to leave you with a slightly more lasting impression of him.

DA MA'S WAY OF TALKING

THE MATCHMAKER

THE APPRENTICE
THE FOOTBALL FAN
XIAO LIU
MR. HU, ARE YOU COMING
REEDUCATION
THE WHARF

I still have perfect recall of Li Zi's student number: 3379101. Mine was 3379102. I've often admired the genius of the serial number system: why, another 3379102 probably won't come along for another hundred years. Even if someone two or three generations after me does take my number in 2079, I'll be too dead to be inconvenienced by the potential confusion of identity. And whoever inherits my number will have no idea I ever existed. I'm too much of a mediocrity to make any mark on posterity. Indeed, I'll happily admit that 3379102 is already as good as dead.

During my time at university, I was punished as many times for skipping class, picking fights, and cheating as 3379101 won honors and prizes, so we were unlikely to become friends. The year we graduated, 1983, the Human Resources representatives from various work units visited our department looking for new recruits. Our college had been founded in 1894, and it was one of the best engineering universities in the country. Li Zi was a first-class student—a class monitor, no less, and a party member, of course. In 1983, he was clearly the star of our cohort and destined for great things. So I owe special thanks here to our chain-smoking, balding tutor, who decided to throw me, 3379102, in with the stellar Li Zi as a free bonus and send the pair of us to a new company that manufactured setups for power stations. I managed to swing the deal only because our teacher was a smoker. If he'd had another weakness—for the opposite sex, for example—I would have had a harder time fixing it.

Our former star student spent his first six months in the world of work in something of a depression. From time to time, he'd knock on the door of my dorm in the middle of the night for a chat: "All that studying: what a fucking waste of time." I knew that he was saying that only to ingratiate himself with me; I, for one, took the opposite view. But Li Zi was clever, and from Jiangnan, too—a region long famous for producing China's smartest operators. Soon enough, he'd found his place in the industrial machine and stopped seeking me out. If anything, we became even less friendly with each other than we had been at college. After my old classmate became the departmental manager, some of my colleagues saw me as a conduit to Li Zi. For their sakes alone, I went asking for favors from him. Every time, Li Zi satisfied my clients' demands. He had never been someone with particularly strong principles. But far from acquiring a new sense of grateful affection for my classmate, I wanted to see even less of him.

It was only in the last year or two that Li Zi and I started to get friendly—almost ten years after we graduated. Over this decade, Li Zi had had his appendix, his tonsils, his gallbladder, and his foreskin removed, and he had lost twenty-five pounds. After all this, I began to feel things were a little more even, as if we were better matched than we had originally been as classmates. So I slowly started to see more of him. His child's third word—imagine, four years old and only three words—was "uncle." I had a hidden talent for producing sweets out of thin air, you see.

Though I should probably tell you right now that this wasn't the whole story.

*

When Li Zi and I were together, he did most of the talking. He was good at it, and it brought him pleasure, too. Once a class monitor, always a class monitor; he seemed set on keeping an eye on my moral and social well-being for the rest of our lives. Ten years later, Li Zi's perorations had become even wordier, even more long-winded than they had been at college, but they didn't bother me, truly, because I wasn't listening. Whom had I listened to over the years? No one, which was why I was in the mess I found myself in now. While Li Zi was passionately holding forth, his wife Wang Qing would usually bring us something to eat, and I would obediently swallow it down. Not with unseemly greed, of course, but steadily and methodically. In fact, the rhythms of my chewing synchronized exactly with those of Li Zi's speech. But there were limits to my former classmate's generosity (though he liked to be generous when the situation required it), so if he wasn't in the mood to watch three pounds of sugar-roasted chestnuts disappear down my throat, he tended to shut up.

"Male graduate, thirty, unmarried. No congenital defects, no bad habits. Seeks a modest, respectable young woman for companionship. Will swap photographs but no unsolicited visits."

This was the first draft of my personal ad as authored by Li Zi. He'd first insisted that I take out the ad and then on writing it himself. The expression on his dry, sallow face was intolerant of argument, dictatorial even. Giving him the benefit of the doubt, I decided to view the whole episode as articulating a class monitor's sense of responsibility to a subordinate. This trivial scrap of text had had a strangely animating effect on him, rather like the transformer robot that had so excited his idiot daughter when I'd given it to her, even though she couldn't figure out how to play with it. He shouted several times for Wang Qing to come and read it. Look, the subtext clearly ran, what a wonderful paragraph your husband Li Zi, with his first-class degree, has written.

Wang Qing took a very long time to emerge and eventually did so with very poor grace. When I was there, she avoided appearing if she possibly could or if she did come out, she always had a sour expression on her face. If I'd been the type to take offense, it would have been quite easy to interpret her inhospitality as an expression of contempt for me. Standing next to Li Zi, she leaned slightly to the right. Wang Qing's pink, healthy complexion cast Li Zi's aging grayness into greater relief. Standing next to each other, they were two contrasting sides of the same coin. At that moment, I felt strangely like the person tossing that coin—even while there was no logic for this feeling. Why, at that moment, *I* was Li Zi's plaything—his project.

"What do you think about this bit?" Li Zi asked his wife earnestly. "I'm not sure about it."

"Huh?" His wife had already wandered off to see to her daughter—offspring of a first-class student and a fine pair of childbearing hips—who was lying on her back like a beetle, unable to right herself.

"Is 'young woman' narrowing the field too much? And . . ." He turned back toward me: impatient with the problem but also looking slightly embarrassed. Wang Qing turned in the same direction but without focusing on me. I looked up at both of them, deliberately displaying the pitiful signs of my premature aging: my receding hairline, my lined forehead. Then I gazed uninhibitedly at the more attractive half of the couple. Out of the corner of my eye, somewhere to my right, I noticed a pale-colored thing take a fall. Wang Qing rushed over. I resigned myself to looking back at Li Zi.

"How about we say 'divorced but no children' . . . because . . ." Li Zi edged his chair over toward me as if he really wanted to know what I thought.

"She could have ten children for all I care. It'll save me the trouble."

"Don't you think he's setting his sights a little low?" Li Zi looked back at Wang Qing. "Where there's a will, there's a way. Or if you can't find anyone, we can always get a girl from the countryside. That way, you might even find yourself an eighteen-year-old. I'll get her a job . . ." Wang Qing scooped up their daughter and placed her on his father's lap so she wouldn't fall off again.

“No. I definitely want someone who’s already been married.”

“All right.” Li Zi crossed out “modest, respectable young woman” with his fountain pen and wrote over the top “divorced, with or without children, any number acceptable.” As Wang Qing turned to leave again, Li Zi quickly stopped her. “We’re not done yet.” He turned back toward me.

“How about twice divorced? I mean, as long as she . . .”

“Sure,” I swiftly interrupted him. “A woman’s like a boiler, right? If it worked in the past, it’ll work again—just needs a bit of maintenance.” Li Zi had the grace to look a little abashed. “No, no, that’s not what I meant,” he quickly said. Wang Qing topped up our cups of tea. She seemed to feel rather superfluous in the situation and thought she might as well fill my cup while she was performing the service for her husband.

“Whatever. You can’t be too picky at my age,” I told my old classmate.

“Now, that’s no way to talk.” Putting on his serious, team-leader face, Li Zi concentrated on his amendments. His daughter craned round to the right to peek at what he was writing—farther and farther until she lost her balance and fell between his legs. Li Zi ignored her.

His masterpiece completed, he passed it to me to read, contentedly replacing the pen in his breast pocket. He actually wrote rather beautifully with a fountain pen; he’d copied out several calligraphy manuals to improve his handwriting. He favored the imitation Song style—at least I think it was that. He made a fair copy of my personal ad: “Male graduate, thirty, unmarried. No congenital defects, no bad habits. Seeks a divorced woman, any number of times acceptable, with or without children, any number acceptable. Will swap photographs.” But while I was still savoring this glowing write-up, Li Zi suddenly leaned forward, snatched it from me, thrust it at Wang Qing, and told her to read it. She was brushing the dust off her daughter’s bottom.

“Why’re you showing it to me?” Wang Qing snapped as she scooped up her daughter and left the room. The brief flicker of excitement on Li Zi’s face faded, giving way to disappointment.

“It’s perfect,” I said. “I’ll take it to the newspaper office tomorrow.”

"No, it'll never work," Li Zi said. He carefully tore it into pieces and threw the whole thing into the bin. He smiled at me, seeming a little out of breath. It was time for me to go, I realized.

*

I don't want to get married; I just want to sleep with women from time to time. Well, that's how I feel at the moment, anyway. I never make trouble for the other party, and I hope that she'll return the favor. Even bandits have their own code. I didn't start out with this plan, but this is just how things have turned out over the years. I set myself three rules of engagement: don't make any promises, don't get involved with married women, and never get mixed up with virgins. These aren't set in stone, but it's good to have at least a theoretical framework of best practice. I have an unusually low opinion of myself. It didn't bother me until it was too late, until I became a conscious adult and realized that everyone else shared my view. And the only women willing to be around me I tended to have a low opinion of, too. That way it was more relaxing for everyone involved—no one felt demeaned by the encounter.

But for the past couple of years, my private life has settled into a routine. I'm no sex addict; I'm satisfied with very little. (And in any case, I'm not physically what I once was, although I'm in good shape compared with my old friend 3379101.) My current special friend is twenty-eight, from Wafangdian in Liaoning in the northeast and, to my enormous regret, married. We agree on everything except about my low self-esteem, and that's probably only because she felt it reflected badly on her. Our first encounter took place two autumns ago; I could feel the tension in her—her buttocks were as taut as a basketball. (I should know; I was center forward on my high school basketball team.) She sat up in bed as soon as we were done and began to cry. I sensed this was a ritual that I'd just have to get used to. When she wouldn't stop, I had no choice but to go against the habit of a lifetime and try and comfort her. I hated myself for my hypocrisy. But she finally did stop crying, thank heavens. She wiped away her tears and asked if we could do it again. "Best not," I replied.

Back then, I was still living in the dorm at my electrical engineering company because I wasn't married. In order to keep things quiet from my roommates, I rented a small apartment—a sitting room and a bedroom—in a residential development called Carefree Compound. The rent was 150 a month, and we split it fifty-fifty. She insisted on paying her share, maybe to stop me bringing other women there (except with her approval). Seventy-five *yuan* was not a small sum, and I had huge admiration for her ability to produce her share of the rent month after month: her housekeeping skills must have been extraordinary. I wanted to do what I could for her, but I was a very limited person. To me, tobacco was more important than women: it had ruined my teeth, my sense of smell, my basketball player's physique, my appetite, my libido. It had enslaved me totally. Because women had so little power over me, I couldn't bring myself to depend on them. I had a kind of hardwired wariness toward them. I could never relax around them—I found them painfully unsettling. I inherited this sense of wariness from my father; he, too, was invulnerable to women—it was his political beliefs that had destroyed him, just as tobacco had ruined me.

So let me describe this woman in the only language that I properly understood: she was a top-quality domestic product—a Yuxi Yunnan cigarette, golden yellow tobacco, middle tar. Nice enough to look at but with a bitter aftertaste.

As soon as she stepped into our seventh-floor apartment, she became Vivien Leigh—well, the Vivien Leigh who played Scarlet O'Hara in *Gone with the Wind*. Naturally, that left me with little choice but to play Clark Gable playing Rhett Butler, the toy of an older woman who goes on to toy with younger women after he makes his fortune. We didn't always role-play—it was only when we were in particularly high spirits. Though I knew that I wasn't a particularly appropriate choice to play Clark Gable, I felt that she was an even poorer fit for Vivien Leigh. Let me emphasize, though, that we took to impersonating the stars of the silver screen not out of vanity but purely out of habit.

Near the start of our relationship, she asked, then later ordered, me not to smoke in bed. Not a big thing to ask, you might think. But I just couldn't do it; without cigarettes, I lacked the energy for this kind of thing. I had to have them. The first time I broke her rule, she snatched the cigarette out of my mouth and threw it to one side of the bed, but as soon as she saw the consequences of her actions, she had no choice but to pick up the cigarette and give it back to me. When I then asked her to light it for me as well, I think that she probably saw the writing on the wall for her place in our relationship. But she refused to submit outright to my own degeneracy; she found her own way to inject energy into our encounters. It was around this time that we saw *Gone with the Wind* (with tickets issued from work), so she suggested that we try reenacting it in the comfort of our adulterous nest. This struck me as an excellent idea, since we were both heartily sick of our respective realities.

Over the course of time, we began to enjoy the extracurricular drama practice, and it became more of a regular thing. She loved it when I called her Vivien Leigh. I must confess I wasn't very excited about the whole Clark Gable thing, but I was happy to give it a try—it distracted me temporarily from my cigarettes. Maybe I'd been acting all my life, and I just didn't know it. In any case, I got the strong sense that all she really cared about was that I acclaimed her interpretation of Vivien Leigh. She'd told me that at primary school she'd been the head of the Cultural Recreation Propaganda Team and had learned to play the dulcimer. While at high school, she'd tried, but failed, to get into the Liaoning Provincial Song and Dance Delegation. She'd kept up her interest at university, becoming a dancer in the College Arts Troupe, with a particular flair for aerobics (I suspected her interest had faded since graduation). She was often generous in her praise for my own performances; the first time I completed my impersonation of Rhett Butler, she sprang off the bed in ecstasies, the sweat pouring off her, and told me I was a real natural.

In addition to *Gone with the Wind,* we also often did *Love Story, The Cassandra Crossing,* and *Waterloo Bridge.* We performed them all so many times that I imagined her eyes had turned as blue as their heroines'. When we were feeling less ebullient, *Romeo and Juliet* suited. Though personally I felt that *Hamlet* showcased my acting talents the best. The day we were scheduled to do the prince of Denmark for the first time, she arrived half an hour late and in a state of great excitement because she had in her bag a copy of *Selected Plays of Shakespeare*. We never did much extemporizing. But like all great actors, I had my little eccentricities. If I wasn't in the mood, I'd refuse to take to the stage. Vivien Leigh couldn't understand why we couldn't unwind by reading out loud a couple of scenes from the play, to while away a winter's afternoon. "All right," I said, "I'll play a part. Today, I want to be your husband, the father of your child." She snatched up her bag and stormed out of the apartment.

✶

Meantime, Li Zi had been diligently informing all our surviving classmates about 3379102's abject personal circumstances. His broadcasting technique consisted of appealing to any of our classmates with a grain of conscience to take pity on my (solitary) situation and to keep an eye out for potential matches. This latest endeavor destroyed any residual sense of superiority that I still felt from having remained a bachelor. For the first time, I began to feel that to be unmarried at thirty was a mistake, another punishment for my undergraduate misdeeds. I'd made more than my fair share of enemies during my four years at university, and so I was deeply moved by how willing my old classmates were to bury the hatchet and express their sympathies. But once I'd got over my gratitude, what I wanted to do more than anything was to throw my old class monitor, and now departmental manager, out of the nearest window. After having dinner in the company cafeteria, I chose to forgo a visit to Carefree Compound (where I knew my Chinese Vivien Leigh was awaiting her supporting actor). Li Zi and I needed to talk.

"I was just about to go looking for you myself." He seemed delighted to see me, which was an unexpected bonus. I was instructed to sit down on the sofa; a half-empty packet of cigarettes lay on the coffee table before me. Yet another unexpected bonus, since Li Zi didn't smoke himself. Naturally, he usually had cigarettes around the house but never such a good brand as this. To place them in front of me in this way meant that he expected every cigarette to be smoked; he knew what I was like. Picking up his cup of tea, he sat opposite me and told me to have a cigarette.

"I came to tell you—"

"Hold on." Li Zi interrupted. Smiling mysteriously, he fished a letter out of his pocket and brandished it at me. His scrawny neck seemed to have stretched even longer—perhaps from excitement. "Guess what this is."

"Look, what I really wanted to talk about was—"

"Hold on," he interrupted a second time, waving the envelope in front of me. "Look at the sender's address first. That's all you can see for the time being." When I reached out for it, he deftly swatted me away. The writing on the envelope was very small; I could make out only the words "Xilinhot." I'd never heard of the place, but neither had I ever planned on making a closer acquaintance with it. Li Zi struck a lunge pose as if readying himself for either attack or defense.

"Xilinhot. What a beautiful word! What does it make you think of?" Li Zi's neck was reminding me more and more of a chicken's, particularly as he had now taken to strutting around the room like a delighted cockerel. Happiness made him forget his various ailments.

It didn't make me think of anything. Xilinhot, to me, was three syllables placed next to each other: Xi, lin, and hot. I tilted my head to one side and drew sharply on my cigarette. Now I understood Li Zi's unusual liberality today. The cigarettes were slightly mildewed—though not so badly that an addict like me would refuse them. My task was to use them up for him. I took another drag; the faintly moldy taste was a perfect accompaniment to a Li Zi lecture.

"Honestly." Li Zi was deeply disappointed by my poor memory. The tip of his nose glistened slightly, a beacon of light in his dull, peaky face. He took a disgruntled sip of tea and then chewed the tea leaves marooned in his mouth. It was a habit of his. Once he'd swallowed the carefully masticated leaves, he deigned to jog my memory: "Liu . . . Jia . . . lan," he spelled out in a low voice.

Another random sound string. However, after a little more patient prompting from Li Zi, it finally came back to me: yes, I'd once had a classmate called Liu Jialan. A short, thin girl.

*

So: Liu Jialan had written a letter to her former class monitor. Her text oozed with nostalgia for our college days, the nostalgia of an unmarried thirty-something woman. At the end, she asked Li Zi to pass on her best wishes to 3379102, and that was all there was to it. But it was more than that, of course: she also represented an elevated statistical probability of romantic success, which was probably the cause of Li Zi's elation. Although cigarettes had dulled my sense of smell to almost nothing, I could still just about scent what was going on here—even if I took no interest in it. Actually, that was not quite true. Inside, I was swearing blind at Li Zi, who had, it seemed, succeeded in broadcasting across thousands of miles, all the way up to Xilinhot in Inner Mongolia, exactly how pathetic I was.

"Look, Li Zi, what I came over today to say was–"

"Calm down, calm down. Have another cigarette." Li Zi leaned back, loosening his belt. He had a narrow, wasplike waist—narrow enough to carry off a skirt. I didn't know what had made him feel bloated all of a sudden.

"You don't have to go blabbing about me to so many people. I don't need your help."

Li Zi smiled, nodding his head repeatedly. There was no real humor to his smile; it was only so many frozen lines etched onto his face. I lit a cigarette and bent forward to smoke it, to concentrate on the taste. He was still nodding as if he needed someone to tell him to stop.

"Listen." His eyes suddenly lit up, and he wagged a finger at me. "You're forgetting something." He left a portentous pause, waiting for me to look up; I could think of no reason to do so. This left him no choice but to finish his point.

"Liu Jialan's still young!" I understood Li Zi too well: "still young" was code for virgin. In Li Zi's curious view, the hymen wasn't a part of the body; it was a part of the soul. Perhaps in his mind, it was even more important than all those body parts he had discarded over the past ten years. However hard I tried to stay angry, I had to laugh.

"Look at it this way," I told him. "I grew up in Quanzhou, a port on the east coast. After the Opium War, it was closed off to the outside world and the harbor silted up. The city went into decline while the nearby island of Xiamen prospered. All that's left of the old harbor now is a single stone tablet, with the inscription 'The Ruins of Quanzhou Bay.'"

Animated by my metaphor, Li Zi began rebutting it even before he'd finished chewing on his current mouthful of tea leaves.

"Liu Jialan's nothing like that stone memorial." He spat out his half-masticated tea leaves in order to make his point more forcefully. "Quanzhou declined because of the Qing government's corruption. Where there's a will, there's a way; it could easily become a thriving commercial hub again."

"Or I could just try my luck in Xiamen."

"Xiamen's too far away. You'd be better off sticking with Quanzhou. After all, time waits for no man."

"In a country as big as China, there'll always be new Xiamens."

We were still passionately debating my analogy when Wang Qing got home, looking exhausted after her overtime (inevitably, Li Zi ended up winning me over). Wang Qing would have doubtless blamed me for dragging her husband into a pointless geographical argument about the respective merits of Quanzhou and Xiamen. As she set her bag down, she deliberately knocked over the washstand, probably hoping that the clatter would drive me away. I'm sensitive to other people like that. I wondered if I could stretch my analogy a little further. To Li Zi, Wang Qing was no Quanzhou, but Li Zi assuredly represented the corrupt late Qing government to Wang Qing. "I'd better be going," I said. Just as I was leaving, I remembered why I'd come in the first place. "You really don't need to bother about me," I reiterated to my former classmate. "Please."

*

I came to my senses when my relationship with the married woman drifted into its third year. It wasn't right, I told her; it was an unequal business transaction. Vivien Leigh began to cry: she'd pay more than half of the rent for the Carefree Compound or even all of it. That wasn't what I meant, of course. And for her to respond in this way make me feel even more strongly that the whole thing really was a kind of business transaction to her. I was a free gift thrown in with her husband like a male dowry, just as 3379102 had been a bonus extra thrown in with 3379101. Her husband wasn't enough for her, so she'd latched onto me to make up the slack. I hoped we'd be able to part amicably: she could go on being a dutiful wife and mother while I could carry on being the low-grade human being I was.

Near the start of each assignation, she now took to tormenting me by threatening to divorce her husband so she could marry me. The declaration would throw me into a panic: I'd beg her to abandon such an idiotic notion. She'd then get me to say my lines, and I'd have to do my best to get into the part so as to distract her. On those days, I'd be lucky if I got away with doing only Romeo. For a while, I got truly sick of acting—or of acting a part for her. I began to feel terrible, as though I were always a bit part in a bigger drama. By day I was a wage slave; by night, I had to entertain another keeper. But one exhausted Sunday morning, I suddenly saw a solution to my problem. "I can't wait for you any longer," Rhett Butler exclaimed, clasping Scarlet O'Hara's hand. "Marry me!"

That gave me a significant tactical advantage. She dropped the subject of marriage altogether; she'd obviously never meant it. Vivien Leigh now abandoned the big-star act and took on the more limited role that I was offering her. We went on for another year like this.

SCENE: A ROOM IN THE CASTLE.

Hamlet enters stage right dressed only in a pair of baggy running shorts with a faded number 10 printed on the seat; he has a cigarette in his mouth.

OPHELIA (*solidly built, wearing an outsized, slightly grubby man's T-shirt*): Since when did Hamlet smoke?

HAMLET: Why shouldn't he? Come on, get on with it (*takes a long draw and slowly exhales*). Lady, shall I lie in your lap?

OPHELIA: No, my lord.

HAMLET: I mean, my head upon your lap?

OPHELIA: Ay, my lord.

HAMLET: Do you think I meant country matters?

OPHELIA: I think nothing, my lord (*removes the cigarette butt from Hamlet's mouth*).

HAMLET: That's a fair thought to lie between maids' legs.

OPHELIA: What is, my lord?

HAMLET: Nothing.

OPHELIA (*guiding Hamlet's repellently nicotine-stained index finger inside her T-shirt*): You are merry, my lord.

HAMLET: Who, I?

OPHELIA: Ay, my lord.

HAMLET: O God, your only jig maker. What should a man do
but be merry? For look you, how cheerfully my
mother looks, and my father died within these two hours.

✶

For this deathless performance, we used Zhu Shenghao's authoritative Chinese translation, I seem to recall. In a rehearsal break, Hamlet requested that Ophelia focus on a single, simple fact: in the two years since they'd taken up with each other, he hadn't seen one other woman, even though she could have her husband whenever she wanted. Was that fair, was that equal? Ophelia thought it through: "Give me some time, and I'll sort things out."

✶

One afternoon a couple of weeks later, Li Zi called me just before I was supposed to be leaving work. He wanted me to come to his place right away—for dinner. I wasn't too fond of having dinner at his place because Wang Qing's cooking was no better than the food I could get in the staff cafeteria. Another problem was that the quantity and choice of dishes were decided exclusively by Li Zi. And he tended to hope that the glow of friendship and fond remembrance of times past would compensate for the lack of culinary abundance. Of course, I had no way of wriggling out of it; our ten years of acquaintance had left me bereft of excuses.

Not far from the main company building was the College of Geology. If you stood on the top floor of the building, you could see the college's basketball court. After finishing work, I'd often light a cigarette and stand there, watching the students play basketball until it got dark. It was usually boys playing—half a match or so. Occasionally, girls played too. They weren't so aggressive in their tackling and dribbling, but they did scream a lot. I couldn't make out their faces from this distance, but I enjoyed the colorful clothes they wore and the way they chased after the ball. Youth is a beautiful thing.

After my fourth cigarette, I ambled off to Li Zi's place. Even so, I was worried I was going to be too early: Wang Qing always took an age to serve dinner while Li Zi filled in the gap with one or another of his sermons. The evening ahead held out little appeal.

When Li Zi opened the door—wearing a symbolic white apron—his eyes lit up: "He's here at last." I was a little nonplussed—I felt like quarry that had fallen into a hunter's trap. My instincts were right. As I came in, a slightly built woman in a black dress on the sofa in the sitting room stood up and smiled at me. I knew instantly who she was: Liu Jialan, all the way from Xilinhot. Li Zi flounced triumphantly off into the kitchen, like someone who had just set two fighting crickets against each other and wanted to leave the battle arena as soon as possible. The show was about to begin.

After a little small talk, silence descended between us. Wang Qing bustled out of the kitchen and uncovered the tray of nuts and dried fruit in front of Liu Jialan. "Why aren't you looking after the guest?" she scolded me. She smiled at me, a rare privilege indeed. I knew that Wang Qing was enjoying witnessing my discomfort.

I finally stumbled onto a topic of conversation: "I'm trying to remember . . . your student number . . ." Over in the kitchen, Li Zi was deliberately keeping his back to me, but I could sense that he was following my every word with oppressive concentration.

"My student number?" Liu Jialan frowned with surprise at the question; two fine lines appeared on her forehead.

"Mine was 3379102, Li Zi's was—"

"Oh. Mine was 3379125." She was a little red around the eyes; she reminded me of an exhausted, underweight rabbit that had wandered too far from home. She must have come straight to Li Zi's house from the train. She'd traveled all the way from Xilinhot to resolve a problem left over from ten years ago.

Liu Jialan sat next to me during dinner. She didn't say much. Wang Qing was much more talkative than normal and kept on helping Liu Jialan to food while endlessly enumerating my faults. After drinking a little wine, Liu Jialan flushed crimson. She looked much younger than Li Zi or I did, but the last ten years had robbed her of her appetite for talk. Both physically and psychologically, the passage of time seemed to have shrunk her.

✶

Picking up on a not-so-subtle hint from Li Zi after dinner, I took Liu Jialan out for a stroll. Still disinclined to talk, she walked behind me, carrying her own bag. When I suggested I take it for her, Liu Jialan insisted she was fine. We stood under the stop for the number 5 bus, with perhaps three feet between us, looking out over the opposite side of the road. A filthy, disheveled migrant laborer asked her for directions; Liu Jialan silently looked to me. There was something strange, remote, about her gaze, which quickly glanced off me and onto the empty space in front of me. I quickly stepped forward to give him directions. After the stranger had moved off, I felt awkward returning to the spot I'd previously occupied. She stood next to me, often looking up at the stars. I realized that she was someone still full of hope about the future—this was what seemed so alien to me. Surrounded by the rush of vehicles, pedestrians, the still vibrating streetcar lines, I felt myself grow tense and quickly lit a cigarette.

The number 5 bus terminated at Hanzhong Gate: cross one more bridge and you ended up at Carefree Compound. We stood where two carriages were joined; despite the tremors of the vehicle, she maintained a steady, straight posture. When the bus swerved to one side, she leaned toward me and then immediately righted herself again. Her elbow rested below mine: it struck me as unusually pointed—like the look that she had thrown at me when we were waiting for the bus.

"So what have you been doing with yourself all these years?" Liu Jialan smoothed a few stray hairs from her forehead with her right palm, her face now illuminated, now in shadow.

"Nothing much." I grabbed with my right hand for the bar above my head but struggled to keep my balance—at one point, she even had to reach out to steady me.

"Your center of gravity is too high." She smiled. There was something very youthful about her smile, which came very slowly to her face.

"How about you?" I put my hand in my pocket and squeezed my packet of cigarettes. I had two, no three, left.

"Me? Oh, I took something of a wrong turn. I thought that I should try to be like a man in all things." She glanced briefly up at me and then wryly continued. "And now I've learned that I'm not a man after all. I'm a woman."

The bus stopped again, and a few more people got on. One of them stood half interposed between us, his back to me. We stopped talking. After the conductor had finished selling tickets, he turned the light off and the bus fell silent again. I couldn't make her face out clearly, but I knew she was looking at me. I turned to look out of the window. I had forgotten where the bus was going. Eventually I heard her say something else—as if she were talking to herself.

"Back at university, I'd always thought . . . that you were a bit different from the rest of them."

I put a cigarette in my mouth and pulled out my lighter. After two fumbled attempts, I failed to light up. "Please don't smoke on the bus," a woman screeched from somewhere behind me. I turned around but couldn't work out who had spoken; every face was in shadow. I replaced the lighter in my pocket but left the cigarette in my mouth. The bus stopped again. This time, a great many people got on, apparently in a group—from their accent, I guessed they were a crowd of rural laborers from north Jiangsu. Liu Jialan and I were now completely separated; I was pushed closer and closer to the door. I glanced outside the window: within a few stops we'd be at the terminus of line 5.

At the stop before Hanzhong Gate, I got off, alone. I could sense Liu Jialan looking at me from out of the window. But I couldn't see anything inside the vehicle. Because the bus had been so crowded, the cigarette in my mouth had broken in half. I felt a twinge of regret.

✶

"We'll have to be quick today, it's my turn to do the nursery pickup." Vivien Leigh threw down her bag as she spoke; her coat was off by the end of the sentence. I took two sharp draws on my cigarette; I needed them. I'd once sketched, on the back of the cutaway view of an oil pump, the pyramid of her life: her child was at the tip, her husband somewhere on the slope; I languished at the foot of the structure. She divided her time logically and inflexibly according to this schema, and that was how she had been able to juggle the situation so skillfully over the past few years. Every problem, she felt, had a reasonable solution. I took another couple of drags; she no longer tried to stop me—she understood my limitations.

HAMLET: Are you honest? (*After one last drag, he throws his cigarette to the floor.*)

OPHELIA (*removing two outer layers with difficulty*): My lord?

HAMLET (*despite his irritation with the situation, giving her a hand with her jumper*): Are you fair?

OPHELIA: What means your lordship?

HAMLET (*examining her nails, of which he is inordinately afraid; they have been very brutal to him in the past*):
That if you be honest and fair, your honesty should
admit no discourse to your beauty.

OPHELIA: Could beauty, my lord, have better commerce than with honesty? (*She prods at his penis, then takes a sip of tea from a cup on the table.*)

HAMLET: Ay, truly; for the power of beauty will sooner transform honesty from what it is to a bawd than the force of honesty can translate beauty into his likeness: this was sometime a paradox, but now the time gives it proof. (*A torrent of cold tea pours down his front; he looks ridiculous.*) I did love you once.

She pulled me inside her, but it was no good—she was in too much of a hurry. I decided I hated this life I was living. I felt as if I was always on the periphery of my own life. I was thirty years old: however low caliber I was, I still deserved to lead a normal life.

Vivien Leigh burst into tears again. I didn't know why she was crying; I could make less and less sense of her. There was no love between us; there never would be. "What if I divorced my husband and married you right away?" she suggested again. I lit a cigarette; getting married had never been part of the plan. I'd always been honest with her about that.

*

Another week passed calmly enough. She went back to being a devoted wife and mother. I asked her to meet me in Carefree Compound one last time, because I was planning to let the tenancy lapse. Although she fought the idea, I'd made up my mind. For two years, I'd given up other women for her; I felt like I was sickening for them. I had no doubt about what I should do.

"Aren't you afraid I've already asked for a divorce?" She seemed to be threatening me.

"If you don't seem worried, why should I be worried?"

"You don't know me." She really was threatening me.

"All right, since you brought up the subject. Although I never planned to marry you, if you get a divorce, I'll marry you."

After the tenancy lapsed, I planned to move back into my dorm. She wouldn't dare visit me there, and even if she did come, she'd have to keep quiet. Soon enough, we stopped seeing each other. I was already busy thinking about my future: I'd reaffirmed my commitment to my three basic rules of engagement. I had to, for the sake of self-preservation.

All Vivien Leigh could do was weep. I felt that she was like a child crying over a lost toy. Was I being unfair? I didn't think so. I suggested that before the tenancy lapsed, we might as well have one last farewell performance. Initially reluctant to agree, she finally caved in, through lack of self-control. She couldn't resist taking the stage one last time. You should love life and treasure youth, she was always telling me. I had to admit that that evening was perhaps her best performance ever.

QUEEN GERTRUDE: O Hamlet, thou hast cleft my heart in twain (*weeping and gazing mournfully at the sky*).

HAMLET: O, throw away the worser part of it,
And live the purer with the other half.
Good night: but go not to mine uncle's bed;
Assume a virtue, if you have it not.
That monster, custom, who all sense doth eat,
Of habits devil, is angel yet in this,
That to the use of actions fair and good
He likewise gives a frock or livery,
That aptly is put on.

But Queen Gertrude had the last word: "We're not finished yet." Hamlet was unsettled; it took several drags on his cigarette to calm him down.

✶

The next morning, Li Zi turned up as soon as I got to work. He shook his head impatiently at me; all my colleagues heard his heavy, theatrical sighs. I reluctantly followed him into his office. He took a couple of cigarettes out of a black box, laid them on the table, and then looked long and hard at me. What right did he have to do that? "She brought these for you. So I'm delivering them." Li Zi's expression was unforgiving as if he were forwarding a last will and testament—the last will and testament of a woman past the first flush of youth, leaving a bequest to a total stranger. Was I being unfair? I had no idea; all I could think was that none of them had reason to think they had the right to destroy my inner tranquillity like this. I was too used to the idea that I was a pile of junk that anyone in their right mind would go out of their way to avoid.

"Please give the cigarettes back. I don't need them." I turned to go.

"She's already left. I can't give them back." Li Zi was shouting now.

"Keep them for yourself, then." I opened the door.

"You're a bloody pain, you know that?" Li Zi's Jiangnan accent became thicker whenever he swore, so I didn't catch his exact words—but I guessed he meant something like that.

I had to turn back at this and stood before him. He retreated half a pace.

"You started all this."

Li Zi face seemed suddenly to collapse. He watched me head for the door again, but just as I was about to exit, he told me to wait. He darted in front of me and shut the door behind us.

"Look, what's done is done. She's come a long way. Xilinhot's practically at the other end of the country. And in the ten years since we graduated . . ." He paced up and down in front of me; I had no idea what he was trying to say. Finally, he managed to keep still: "You're making me look really bad. Just come with me to see her off; her train for Shanghai leaves at 9. It's better than nothing."

"You can see her off on your own."

*

After hitting a few red lights and traffic jams en route, we got to the station at 8:45. Lucky Li Zi was such a big shot: it meant he could authorize our taking a company Santana—back in the 1990s, the Chinese man's BMW. When we arrived, Li Zi charged off to buy a couple of platform tickets while I followed behind, Liu Jialan's two gift-wrapped boxes of cigarettes under my arm. By the time we got on to the platform, it was 8:50. We were early: still waiting to have their tickets checked, the passengers weren't on the platform yet. The track itself was thronged with those come to see them off. So there were only the two of us on platform 4: one tall, one short, both looking around them, but not for a train. We were utterly ridiculous. The whole situation made me want to do just one thing: eat the person standing next to me. Perhaps sensing this, Li Zi was eyeing me uneasily.

A mass of people surged out of the mouth of the tunnel and toward us, carrying great bundles of luggage. In an instant, the platform was awash with humanity, but we couldn't spot the one person we were looking for. Li Zi told me to stay where I was while he went searching through the crowds. The train still hadn't come into the station. The weather that day was ideal for Li Zi's purposes: the kind of overcast, sepia conditions that lent themselves perfectly to performing a tear-jerking farewell. The train drew to a halt by the platform, and the passengers surged on. Li Zi wandered back dejectedly; the director had lost his leading lady. We'd better stay where we were, Li Zi said. Maybe she'd changed her mind. "A fascinating possibility," I observed with a dry laugh. I craved a smoke.

Just when I'd found the lighter at the bottom of my pocket, I felt the barrel of a gun in the small of my back. "Freeze!" Li Zi and I turned round; it was Liu Jialan. She maintained her posture: slightly crouched, gun in hand. She looked the same as always. Except this time, she just happened to be holding a gun. For the first time in more than ten years, I studied her in daylight: her short hair, pale skin, the air of extreme competence that she emanated. Was she pretty? Yes, now that I looked properly at her, she was very pretty. Li Zi stood to one side, desperately trying to smile, his face creasing up like a crumpled rose. I was finding the situation stifling.

"I thought maybe you weren't actually leaving," Li Zi said.

"Are you planning to keep me here?" She abandoned her gun-toting pose to adjust the strap on her backpack. It was enormous.

Li Zi laughed mirthlessly; it was the only laugh he was capable of. She didn't look at me. After a pause that seemed to go on forever, I handed back her two boxes of cigarettes. She took them, smiling, then set down her bag, unzipped it, and stuffed them inside. "I don't know where he learned those manners," Li Zi stammered, extremely uneasy at what I'd just done. "No," Liu Jialan said. "I shouldn't have brought them. I wasn't thinking properly."

I had nothing to say. The train was about to leave. First Liu Jialan and Li Zi shook hands, and then she came over and shook hands with me: "Good-bye." Just as she was about to get on the train, she turned round once more, smiled at me, and waved; I waved back. Li Zi seemed to be suffering from delayed reactions; by the time he remembered to wave, she'd disappeared into the train car. I watched as her shoulder straps dug deep into her thin shoulders; maybe she was very tired, I thought. A cigarette was in my right hand, a lighter in my left; I had forgotten all about them.

*

I shared a dorm with a junior translator from the company's foreign affairs department. He was currently in the throes of young love and took a very dim view of my return. I could see his point; I'd been there myself. I often took it upon myself to give him the space that he and his acned girlfriend needed for their afternoons and evenings of ecstasy. But still this was not enough to lessen his simmering resentment of me. He also doubtless felt that someone who remained a bachelor at thirty by definition deserved only contempt, just as the fact that he was young and full of promise was a default source of pride. He left me no choice but to use an old-fashioned method to resolve the issue. In fact, it took only one punch for the whole problem to melt into nothingness. From that point on, we got along famously.

My paramour was right. We weren't finished so easily. Although the promising young interpreter and I had reached a form of tacit understanding over mutual respect of privacy, my affair was in constant danger of being discovered. I begged her to be more prudent: it was the equivalent of risking her life for a taste of puffer fish. I knew that the analogy wasn't right. Even if she'd wanted to try puffer fish, she never would have risked her life for it. Perhaps she was just getting careless—perhaps she didn't want to see the gravity of the situation. I would often try to calm myself with the thought that we were just two piles of flesh experiencing chemical reactions. (Was I being unfair? I no longer knew.) I wanted to forget about her. But eventually she forced me to agree to rent another apartment, to return to the life I had vowed to leave. I was beyond saving. By this point, I also was extremely depressed.

Fortunately, the crisis that was waiting to happen occurred just before it came to this. It was a Wednesday afternoon, I remember. Li Zi called my office, telling me to come around to his place that evening to receive his next sermon on my debased lifestyle. The colleague who took the call said I'd phoned in ill. Since my dorm wasn't far from the office building, Li Zi decided to go over and see me. When he got to the corridor of the sixth floor, he happened to see Wang Qing and me leaving the room together. I was locking the door; Wang Qing's face was still flushed. As I recall, the light that afternoon was particularly limpid. All was quiet around us—everyone was at work. For years, I'd been waiting for this day. I felt an unprecedented sense of release.

> HAMLET: O good Horatio, I'll take the ghost's word for a
> thousand pound. Didst perceive?
> HORATIO: Very well, my lord.

*

I thought about nothing at all for the following week. My appetite was unaffected, and when I was tired, I slept. When my departmental manager called me, my mind remained a blank. I smoked several cigarettes, one after the other, to focus my nervous energy—but all the tension had gone out of me. Only one thought looped round my head: my student number was 3379102, and my alma mater was founded in 1894.

Li Zi was dressed in blue-striped pajamas as if he were sick—his grayish-yellow complexion was a perfect match for his costume. Wang Qing opened the door to me and turned away as soon as she did so; she knew whom to expect. I sat down on the sofa next to Li Zi and saw an unopened packet of cigarettes on the table. Could they have been set out for me? I had no idea. Well, here I was. I felt like I was meeting my former classmate for an assignation at Carefree Compound. Wang

Qing emerged from the kitchen and set a steaming hot cup of tea in front of me. Then she went into the back room where I heard her patiently playing with her daughter. "This is a rabbit; yes, a rabbit. This is a turtle." My student number was 3379102, my alma mater was founded in 1894. I reached for the cigarettes in my pocket. "No," Li Zi told me solemnly. "Smoke these."

A fly was buzzing around the otherwise silent room, spinning a web of noise as delicate as a spider's.

"I haven't been feeling so well lately," Li Zi said softly. I glanced across at him, but he wasn't looking at me. The door to the back room was open, and Wang Qing happened to be diagonally opposite me and clearly visible. Although I wasn't looking in their direction, their daughter, Xiaoqing, stared directly across at me, at her tall uncle. The fly—an enormous bluebottle—buzzed between us. "It's nothing, though," Li Zi seemed to be talking to himself. "Just a cold, a bit of a cold." I stubbed out my cigarette and stared at him. His lip trembled slightly; I thought he was about to go on. He didn't. The fly made a return trip from the opposite end of the room.

Li Zi got up and made for the window. He leaned forward to examine something on the window screen. He felt one corner but failed to discover a hole in it. He then went into the room at the back and returned with a volume of *Reader's Digest*. I had no idea what he was doing, or what he was planning to do. He closed the magazine, took it in his right hand, and then sat back down where he'd been before.

"I'd never imagined, in all good conscience, that . . ." Li Zi's face was expressionless as he spoke. Without finishing his sentence, his right hand (the one holding the magazine) swept the air before my forehead. I jumped slightly at the breeze. The fly was nowhere near.

I brushed the ash off my sleeves and lit another cigarette.

"How old are we now?" He swept the air in front of my forehead, surprising me again. The strain of the movement brought a brief flush to his face. "And now this. Don't you think we're getting on a bit for this sort of thing?"

As I was unable to decipher anything he was saying, I went on smoking. My student number was 3379102, my alma mater was founded in

1894. The foolhardy fly, I noticed, had paused on the window screen; its landing position was illuminated by a pool of lamplight. I could almost make out its eyes. Noticing it too, Li Zi stared silently at it from the sofa. After a while, he abruptly got up and tiptoed over to the window.

He delivered a long premeditated blow. The dust on the window screen billowed up. But the bluebottle survived and now began spinning frantically around Li Zi. It seemed to enrage him: he leaned this way and that, attempting a few more swats, panting roughly as he did so. I'd no idea my old classmate was so agile. Still pursuing the fly, he rushed over in my direction. "Don't move," Li Zi hissed when I looked up. "Whatever you do, don't move."

I obediently looked back down and resumed my smoking posture. I watched as his feet approached, as stealthily as a cat's paws. Then he paused in front of me for what felt like a long time. "Go on, put us out of our misery," I told him. I felt a smart, crisp slap to the head; a line of ash scattered over the floor. My scalp tingled numbly.

HAMLET: To die, to sleep;
To sleep: perchance to dream; ay, there's the rub;
For in that sleep of death what dreams may come
When we have shuffled off this mortal coil,
Must give us pause.

✶

"Wang Qing told me everything. I know exactly what's been going on." Li Zi took a sip of tea. His tone of voice told me he'd slipped back into managerial mode. He seemed very tired and spoke more slowly than usual, which intensified his usual air of self-importance. As I reached down for a cigarette, I glanced at the other room. Wang Qing had her back to me, and that idiot child was still staring at me. What the hell was she playing at?

"You're lucky it was Wang Qing. If it had been anyone else, you'd have been in trouble. Would someone else have been so easy on you—would they have let you stay on at the company afterward?" Li Zi's brow furrowed as if he were plagued by deep heartache. "But Wang Qing's not one to bear grudges. People from the northeast are like that.

"And you're lucky it was me, your old classmate. I understand you. If it had been someone else, someone less forgiving, who knows where things would have ended up." His speech was accompanied by the squeak of tooth on tea leaves. I felt like I was facing off with a ruminating cow—a cow delivering a particularly slow, pompous lecture.

I no longer had any idea what he was saying to me. He was telling me things that seemed utterly alien to my own situation. I went on smoking.

"Wouldn't you agree?"

With what? The cigarette between my fingers drooped; I pulled off the filter. Smoking a filterless cigarette always reminded me of my childhood: of squatting in the latrine pit, a pilfered Flying Horse in my mouth. Time began to melt away disconcertingly before me.

"Everybody has feelings." Li Zi voice now modulated, from C major to a more emotive A minor. "But some just aren't realistic, and you can't force them on other people. You understand this, I'm sure."

I was looking directly at him, at his mouth. It now struck me as a quite wonderful organ. What else was going to come out of it?

"But it's not fair to Wang Qing. She's been worried to death about how to handle it, and that it'll have an effect on our friendship. After all, we go way back. I told her it didn't matter, that she didn't need to worry about me. All she needs to do is avoid giving you any kind of encouragement, to get you to control your own feelings. We can still get along very well, the three of us."

He paused to look at me. He was probably hoping that I would start weeping with gratitude. But that was some way beyond my limited acting skills.

He leaned in. "You haven't had feelings for Wang Qing for ten years, have you?"

Rousing myself, I turned to face him. Wang Qing was staring particularly hard at me; so was her daughter. My throat felt dry; I needed a glass of water.

"So it's just a recent thing. Well, that makes it a bit better." Li Zi lifted his cup and took a sip of tea. "So the feelings can't be that deep. You can get a grip on yourself, can't you?"

Li Zi flipped a tiny mound of tea leaves on his lip into his mouth. I stared: a black, fly-like object meandered its way between his molars and was pitilessly crushed in a series of grating squeaks. From where I was sitting, I could see a muscular bulge along the right-hand side of his face and then the oscillation of his Adam's apple. His gray face fell still once more.

At that instant, right in front of him, I threw up. There on the floor was my dinner: in complete technicolor glory. I made frantic gestures at him.

"You—"

"What about me?"

"Forget it."

*

For three whole months, I've stayed away from Li Zi's place. I probably never will go back there. One day, in the steam combustion workshop, I offered myself up for a work trip that no one else wanted to make. Chifeng in Inner Mongolia wanted to build a power plant near a coalfield, and our workshop manager was worried that he'd be too lonely on his own, so he needed another volunteer. Including travel, the whole trip took four weeks. And just as I was about to leave Chifeng, the company phoned to tell us to go and check on operations in Mianxi, Anshang, and Dandong, in the southeast and the northeast, while we were about it. By the time I was back at work, another two months had passed. After three weary months of exile, I hoped—quite reasonably—that I could start a new life.

Some time after my return, I bumped into my departmental manager in the elevator in the office building. Probably because there were other people around, Li Zi put on this great show of asking how I was. Just so that no one was under any illusions as to where we both stood in the hierarchy: he was my departmental manager—it was his job as my superior to be solicitous. Li Zi's office was on the fourth floor; I worked on the twelfth. This was another clear distinction between us. "I've been looking for you, actually," he said as he was about to get out. "What for?" I asked. "I'll tell you later." He was always very busy with one thing or another.

Another classmate of ours from university days had been allocated a job after graduation in a thermodynamics machinery factory in Xi'an and then moved on to Hainan. Back in college he'd been very similar to me, another lazy, cheating bastard. But he'd somehow struck it rich; I'd heard he kept four or five women in Hainan. Despite this, he still had the energy and the spare cash to organize a class reunion and had invited the entire 33791 cohort to a banquet back at the old place. Everyone had instantly agreed, and it was this that Li Zi wanted to talk to me about: he wanted me to go with him, to make up his entourage. I knew what was going through his mind: to be a departmental manager after ten years was nothing to write home about (because of his health problems, he hadn't done as well as he might have over the last five years). But he was still a departmental manager, and he had to attend this kind of thing. But if he were to go, he would need to take a loser like me to make him look good. I said I'd go.

I might as well. After all, I had been his bonus extra since we left university. If we were going back to college, I might as well carry on the tradition. None of it mattered. I could still remember clearly that my student number was 3379102 and that my alma mater was founded in 1894.

DA MA'S WAY OF TALKI
THE MATCHMAKER

THE APPRENTICE

THE FOOTBALL FA
XIAO LIU
MR. HU, ARE YOU CO
REEDUCATI
THE WHARF

One Wednesday morning, the seven of us—all fresh out of university—were notified that we should go to the office in the transport depot to sign our apprenticeship contracts. I was overjoyed with the factory to which I had chosen to devote my life. I'd done a couple of work placements there while still at college, and I had been delighted by how much the workers swore—and particularly by how freely and foully they expressed their contempt for the upper-level leadership of both the factory and the country as a whole. They liked a drink, too, which struck me as another good thing, since it only increased their already impressive levels of frankness. Since July, I had been eagerly anticipating my elevation to the working class.

Our seven-strong cohort—each of us had graduated from different engineering departments—had been put into a single dorm. We spent the first couple of weeks together at the training center learning about safety regulations. Since the factory was a long way out of the city, there was nowhere for us to go in the evening, so by the end of the first week we knew practically everything there was to know about one another. Here are the bald statistics that emerged: we had among us one Communist Party member, three former student officials, four winners of the State Education Commission Certificate for Undergraduates in English (level 4), one snorer, one teeth grinder, one neurotic, two sports fanatics, one holder of a National Basketball Refereeing Qualification (level 3), two planning to enroll for a PhD after working for a couple of years, one hoping to study abroad, and two with long-distance girlfriends. We were, on the whole, a cagey bunch, unwilling for the time being to declare personal alliances. But we were a special generation all the same, from a very particular context. We'd all taken to the streets during the spring of 1989; we'd all retreated from them in early June. This common ground gave us a greater sense of cohesion, a desire to know what each of us had gone through. And another week of sounding out one another had harvested a second, more intimate data set: two of us had been punished by the university authorities, three had had to retake exams, three had applied to join the party, one had hemorrhoids, two had been unhappy in love, four had smelly feet, one had more generalized body odor issues, one had a relative in the factory, one was a virgin, one had had TB, two suffered from unspecified stomach complaints, one had chronic hepatitis, one had ringworm on his thigh, and two had been circumcised.

By week 3, they were driving me insane. In desperation I rented a ground-floor room, about 215 square feet, in the house of a farmer who lived a couple of stops from the factory. I moved out the evening that my tenancy was accepted. I felt considerably better in my new lodgings—until my landlord's family started to take an oppressive interest in me. But they were the least of my new problems; the absence of a toilet in the house was far more serious. If I needed to relieve myself in the middle of the night, I had to clamber onto a stool (in the dark) and aim (with targeted precision) through the reinforced steel bars over my window. Whenever I varnished the wall opposite in urine, the dog in the farmer's house over the way would wake up and start barking his head off. It was all deeply unrelaxing. Because taking a piss was so problematic, as soon as I settled down to sleep I would start worrying about needing the toilet; the more I worried about it, the greater my desire for the toilet became. Sleep, under these circumstances, eluded me, and I was often late for work.

By the time that I got in that Wednesday, my six peers had already signed their contracts and headed off to the factory floor with their new mentors. "What the hell d'you think you're playing at?" the Human Resources rep barked at me as he searched for my mentor's name. "Mr. Ma's been waiting for you all morning." He stalked off with a brick-like volume of technical accounts under his arm. This encounter took place in one of the factory's small meeting rooms, its walls decorated with a few dusty silk banners, some departmental assessment forms, and a few scrawled solutions to technical issues. In the middle stood an ancient ping-pong table pitted with scratches and cigarette burns. There I waited alone while my mentor and his discolored teeth failed to appear. I decided to tolerate this casual show of arrogance from a vanguard of the proletariat, to let it go. I sat on a badly welded steel chair and leafed through a safety manual.

After half an hour, I began to lose patience. I felt that even the working classes could try to be a bit more punctual. Just then, a short, fat individual—dusty hair, maniacal eyes—appeared in the doorway. Flashing a doltish smile around the room, he muttered that no one was around and moved on. An instant later, he reappeared. "How about a quick game?" he asked. I stared back at him. He gestured at the ping-pong table. It was covered with newspapers; neither net nor paddles were in evidence. "What with?" I asked. Encouraged by my answer, he squatted down by a desk in the corner and extracted two paddles and a ball from the bottom drawer. He rushed out the door again and then quickly returned, hugging to himself an armful of aluminum lunch boxes. Once he had lined them up along the middle of the table, we had a net of sorts. We cleared the newspapers off the table, moved the chairs around it to the edges of the room, and then took up position, paddle in hand, on either side of the table. Faintly uncomfortable with playing ping-pong on my first full day at work, I tried to express my sense of unease to my opponent. He waved his paddle dismissively. "Serve!" Who was I, an apprentice from the bourgeois oppressing classes, to obstruct the will of a veteran proletarian?

After a few rallies, we both began to sweat. My overweight opponent pulled off his shirt, exposing his upper torso in its full flabby glory. I now noted that his neck was also coated in dust: he looked as if he were naked from the waist up except for a black gauze neckerchief. I was a decent amateur player, though a touch rusty. And what my oversized challenger lacked in technical polish, he made up for in chutzpah, so there wasn't actually much to choose between us. Time and again, we slammed the ball into our aluminum net; the impact echoed through the room. A few other employees, whom I had not yet met, stopped by, delighted to chance on a contest. Everyone seemed to know my opponent, or, should I say, they all called him Fat Man and made jokes about his quivering breasts. They asked me what department I was from. Boiler maintenance, I said. "Which work group?" someone wanted to know. "I haven't seen you around." "I'm new," I replied. "I haven't been assigned to a group yet." A murmur rippled through the room: "Ah, a graduate." Even my long anticipated mentor stopped briefly by, a cigarette hanging from his mouth. He seemed pleased to see my opponent. "Hey, Fat Man, just off the night shift?" he shouted, then ambled off without waiting for a reply.

Our audience was very eager that we play a couple of games for points. The fat man said he was too tired. The room was having none of it. If he went straight home, they reasoned, he'd have to see to his wife instead, which would be far more tiring. Or was he afraid of losing? The fat man glanced a little awkwardly in my direction: "How about it?" I nodded quickly and batted the ball over to him. He tapped it back: "You first." So I served. The first game went badly from the start: I quickly lost the ball and then my temper. Although Fat Man's technique wasn't particularly pretty, it did the job. I was determined to show him in the second game what I was made of. But at the end of the first, he set down his paddle on the table. "I really have to get home," he said. "One of you take over for me." The sweat was dripping off his glistening folds of fat. Ignoring his audience's protests, he picked up his shirt and wandered happily off.

I laid down my paddle also; it was time I found my mentor. But before I could leave, an emaciated, wizened old worker tossed away the cigarette butt stuck to his upper lip and took up position on the opposite side of the table. "How about we just tap it back and forth a bit?" he asked, smiling nervously at me. Feeling it rude to refuse such a venerable challenger, I picked up my paddle once more. Whatever my new opponent had said about just warming up, the instant he picked up the paddle, he turned into a crazed alpha male. Irked by my previous jilting at the ping-pong table by the fat man, I unleashed all my fury against my new opponent, playing so hard and fast that he couldn't even get a paddle on the ball. I knew I was overreacting. But my opponent refused to lose his temper, patiently retrieving the ball again and again. After we'd been playing a while, he cleared his larynx into a spittoon by the door. Though his hair was slick with sweat, he seemed determined to go on. I suddenly noticed that my once cheering audience had fallen eerily silent. They seemed edgy for some reason. The tension in the room started to get to me; I decided it was time to bring things to an end. Another couple of uniformed factory workers were hovering in the doorway, volumes of technical regulations—bound in red leather—tucked under their arms. My elderly opponent glanced back at them: "Hold on," he said, "I'll be done in a second." "Come on," one of them—with buck teeth, I remember—urged. "We're all waiting for you." "Just a couple more minutes," my opponent put them off. I fed him a couple of shots, which he gleefully whipped back at me. One of his shots smashed open the boxes across the middle of the table, causing the spoons inside to spill out. I leaned in to tidy them back into line. "Someone else play," I told my audience. "I've had enough."

"No!" came the cry from the opposite end of the table. "You don't think I'm good enough, do you?" My opponent was glaring at me over the lunch boxes. "Of course it's not that," I explained. "But I've been playing for ages now." "It won't hurt you to play a bit longer, then." But my heart just wasn't in it. I shook my head. A tall thin man with a bulging Adam's apple broke the deadlock: "I'll play with you, Liu" (referring, I presumed, to my elderly opponent). Liu turned back to me: "One last game, OK?" "For points?" I asked. He nodded. The tall man winked at me: "Go on then. I'll keep score." I reluctantly took up the paddle again and let my challenger open. As he picked his way diligently through the game, I did my very best not only to make mistakes but also to conceal the fact that I was handicapping myself, and both our scores ascended in orderly fashion. Given my opponent's level of skill, letting him win was no easy thing. But eventually I was victorious: Liu beat me 21 to 19. I felt doubly blessed: released from my travails without having my match fixing exposed. The elderly are like children: those in the middle-age range have a duty of care to keep them happy. To my regret, however, Liu did not seem to be rejoicing. Refusing to look at me, ignoring his colleagues' congratulations, he silently set down his paddle and walked off to the other side of the room. Wiping the sweat off my face with my sleeve, I also laid down my paddle, at which point two new people came over and began hitting the ball back and forth. My white-faced opponent extracted a cigarette, inserted it into his mouth with trembling fingers, and then began searching his pockets for his lighter. The tall thin man, watching him all the while, smartly proffered his own lighter. At which moment, Liu crumpled to the floor with a faint moan.

After a long, surprised pause, the tall man squatted down and rolled Liu over (with some difficulty) onto his back. "Hell," he observed, holding his hand underneath Liu's nose. "I think he's stopped breathing." While everyone else rushed Liu to the factory's clinic, I lagged behind, watching them move farther and farther away until they turned a corner by the steam generator and disappeared from view. I gave up the pursuit. I now found myself on the main road through the factory compound, hemmed in on both sides by high-beamed workshops. Though deserted, the site was heavy with noise. The din was so loud it seemed to have taken physical form—as if I could have lain down on it and floated off. Light-headed with shock, I was desperate to sit down or—better still—to evaporate altogether. A little later, two young female repair workers in filthy, oil-stained overalls emerged from a building to my left and made straight for me along the concrete road. Removing her safety helmet and hooking it over her hand, one of them shook her long coil of hair over her shoulders. A feeling of misery overwhelmed me. I was just starting out on a path that I had chosen; why, then, did I feel so depressed? Their approach finally galvanized me into action. I began walking, faster and faster. But I didn't know where I was going, even after I had exited through the factory's main gate. I was moving—that was all I knew.

I crossed a field full of peanut plants and a small cucumber patch and then entered a house through two wooden doors. An old woman with an egg-sized tumor growing out of her forehead was sitting on a rattan chair in a corner. "What are you doing here?" she asked, looking up at me. Only then did I realize that I'd returned to my lodgings. My landlord's mother was right: I didn't normally come back at midday—I usually had lunch in the factory cafeteria, then a wash in the factory bathhouse and a half-hour lie-down on one of the benches there. I stammered an explanation: I wasn't feeling well, I wanted to go to bed. I passed quickly through the hallway and on to my rented room in the new two-story house in back. The door was open. My landlord, a short, wiry farmer, was sitting on my bed, a cigarette lolling from his mouth, leafing—with obvious enjoyment—through my copy of *The Technologies of Supercritical Electricity Generation*. He seemed too entranced by the book to notice my presence in the doorway. He was squinting through a cloud of smoke; two-thirds of the hand-rolled cigarette in his mouth had burned down into pale ash precariously extended over the butt. I asked him what he was doing. He shuddered with surprise; a snow cloud of cigarette disintegrated over my book. Flicking the residue onto the floor, he stood up, smiling awkwardly: "I was just opening the windows, to air out the room." He made for the exit. I didn't say anything else, mainly because I lacked the strength. After he had carefully closed the door behind him, I pulled back the mat spread over the bed and checked that the one-hundred-*yuan* note I had saved from my first ever paycheck was still quietly curled up where I had left it. Smoothing and refolding it, I put it in my trouser pocket and then lay down, fully dressed.

When I woke, I was surrounded by darkness. I would have turned on my lamp to look at the time, but I couldn't find the switch. I sat up and looked out of the window. All was black outside as well and perfectly silent. Even the drone of the factory had subsided. I wondered if there had been a power outage. Getting up, I groped my way to the door and managed to open it. A dingy orange light was seeping out of the hall in the older part of the house. I gravitated toward it like a moth.

A kerosene lamp sat on a square table in the middle of the room, its lampshade a dusky gray. My landlord was lying in a hammock chair, swinging gently back and forth, fingers interlocked and resting on his concave stomach. His wife was sitting on a stool on the other side of the room, slowly working at some knitting, her hair tightly bound in rollers. My landlord's young daughter was bent over the table doing her homework. I stood stupidly in the doorway, slowly noticing the old lady still sitting quietly in a dark corner. From time to time, she shook out her wrinkly, ostrich-like neck, hung with folds of loose skin.

"Excuse me, could you tell me what time it is?"

Opening his eyes, my landlord looked askance at me and gave a comfortable, lazy sort of smile. His wife closed her eyes. After an expectant pause, she burped very loudly, opened her eyes again, and went on with her knitting. Her daughter looked up and stared, as if mesmerized, by a moth fluttering about the oil lamp. She suddenly opened her mouth, and the moth disappeared in a muffled gulp. The girl looked back down at her homework, chewing squeakily. A strange, bright light shone from the right eye of the old lady—who was seated at an angle to everyone else—then slowly faded. No one answered my question.

"Excuse me, could you tell me what time it is?"

My landlord climbed out of his hammock and stretched, rubbing the sleep dust out of his eyes. "So you're awake, then?" he asked, giving me another slightly embarrassed smile. I nodded. He went on rubbing the dust from his eyes. "You can't have had dinner," he suddenly observed. "Everywhere'll be shut by now—we'll make you something." I said I just wanted to know what time it was. "Don't worry," my landlord ignored me. "It's no trouble." He gestured at his wife to get to work.

Before I could usefully resist, three dishes (featuring half a fish, some pickled soybeans, and fermented tofu) had appeared on the table while my landlady went on clattering in the kitchen. "No, really, no—thank you," I stammered, panic creeping into my voice. But it was too late: my landlady now made a second entrance, carrying a tureen of thick rice porridge. Defeated, I sat down opposite the daughter and bent over the offerings, ambitious to get through them as fast as I could. The old lady tried to struggle out of her chair, unsettled by what was going on. "Is it breakfast time already?" she asked. "He's having his dinner!" my landlady snapped back. "You just had yours! Other people need to eat, too." The old woman fell silent again, except for a series of throaty gurgles.

My landlord lay back down, propping himself up now and again to encourage me to have some more fish. In the hope of avoiding severe food poisoning, I had already spat out the one mouthful I had forced myself to try. It was, I suspected, at least a year old. When my landlord next urged me to have more, I had to tell him straight: the fish was off. He shook his head. "You're not used to the taste, that's all. It's a local specialty."

My chopsticks suddenly encountered a foreign object in the vat of porridge. After dredging it up from the sludge, I discovered it was a hard-boiled egg. I looked up to find my landlord's wife making mysterious eyes at me. Dread prickled my spine. "Egg!" the girl opposite me screeched. In a panic, I put the egg back in the porridge and held it beneath the surface. My landlady glared at her daughter. Glancing back at my landlord, I discovered him in the hammock once more, swinging back and forth with his legs crossed. A moment later, I had the egg again between my chopsticks. Stuffing it into my mouth, I clamped my lips down around it and chewed. Struggling to master a choking sensation, I tried to wash it down with a few mouthfuls of porridge but in so doing discovered several new problems. My heart now racing with fear, I tried to calm myself by surveying the tureen with my chopsticks. If my counting abilities had served me, another four eggs were awaiting me in the depths. My landlord's wife blushed, flashed me an ambiguous smile, then looked away. Inside, I was raging at this infernal hen-woman who had laid five eggs in my bowl. I ate more and more slowly, chewing into submission every tiny mouthful of porridge until I had to stop, because the falling rice level was exposing the eggs. The daughter stood up, keeping her eyes fixed on the bowl. My landlord now came to and, after a dazed, disoriented look around the room, settled his gaze on me. Eventually, the old woman looked round at me too, her wizened lips mouthing something, her pupils emitting a bright, unearthly green light. "You don't have to finish everything if you're full," my landlord's wife quickly conceded. "No," my landlord intervened. "He has to eat it all."

Truly, I did not know what to do. So I threw down my chopsticks, stood up, and, with everyone still staring at me, crossed the room and left by the double wooden doors. Crossing back through the vegetable garden, I picked a baby cucumber, wiped it against my clothes, took a bite (it was bitter), then threw it away. The neighbor's dog—the one I'd never actually seen—began barking, reminding me that I hadn't been to the toilet for hours. As I'd just taken a cucumber, I reckoned, I could pay my hosts back with a spot of free irrigation. The dog set to barking more enthusiastically—though it sounded very close, I couldn't work out where it was. I barked a few times myself, attempting a dialogue of sorts. The dog barked robustly back, so I responded again, this time more aggressively. Another rejoinder came. I now cupped my hands around my mouth, to amplify my next round of howls. The dog responded at a similar volume. But I could tell it was tiring. After a few more exchanges, the dog backed down and stopped responding to my challenges. Anticlimactically, I went on my way.

After walking for about half an hour, I reached the factory dorm; I couldn't think of anywhere else to go. I stood outside the door. Inside, all was silent. Though I still didn't know what time it was, I guessed that my roommates had gone to sleep. My old key wouldn't open the room—it must have been double-locked from the inside. I knocked a couple of times. "Who is it?" someone asked. "Me," I replied. The door opened a crack, to reveal a middle-aged man—in factory uniform—with a goatee. "What d'you want?" he asked. "I live here," I said. He opened the door a crack wider. As soon as I was in, he rebolted the door. The room was thick with curls of smoke. Five very serious-looking men I'd never seen before were sitting around a square table (two desks shoved together) piled with money and playing cards; yet more people, my roommates included, stood behind them. My roommates didn't seem in the least interested in my reappearance, gesturing with silent excitement at the card table. The incandescent light in the center of the room had been blanketed by a newspaper. Its rays were concentrated on the table itself, leaving the rest of the room in shadow. They were playing Tuoguo, a fairly primitive game in which players are dealt pairs of cards. The top card you show to everyone, the bottom one you keep secret, and you bet on the value of the hidden card combined with the open one. My roommate with hemorrhoids suddenly made a move for the door. I asked him where he was going; for a piss, he told me. I needed one, too, I quickly said. In the toilet, I began cautiously interrogating him about how things had been at the factory today. "What d'you mean?" he asked, nonplussed by my question. "Anything—unusual happen?" I expanded a little. "Same old, same old," he told me. I asked for reconfirmation: so, nothing new then? But he was already rushing for the door, before he'd even zipped up his trousers properly. "Nothing ever happens to anyone or anything round here. Except for hemorrhoids," he declared. "We're in the asshole of China," he concluded, warming to his analogy. I followed him back to our room, unable to think of an adequate riposte. Just before we went in, he suddenly turned back to me, a little perturbed. "You didn't go to the toilet." "I changed my mind," I told him.

The game, meantime, was approaching a climax. Two players had gone head to head on a two-hundred-*yuan* stake. After the first showed his cards, the second—a man wearing glasses—raked all the money on the table toward him and then laid out his own hand: a pair of jacks. A collective gasp went round the room. "Show your cards before you take the money, you bastard," growled the loser, a man with a large mole on his lower jawbone. The winner quickly smiled and apologized but now took to singing out his bets—a hundred *yuan* at a time, even when he had a low card on display—trying to bluff his opponents into folding. Although he had picked up only a bit of loose change in the process, psychologically he had everyone else on the run. The next game, he called a hundred before he'd even looked at his pocket card.

"A thousand!" responded the player who'd just complained, the hairs on his mole bristling. The hand holding his cards trembled. His audience immediately tried to talk him out of it. Even the man on the winning streak told him to lower his stakes; he didn't want to match him. The harder everyone tried to dissuade him, the more determined he became. Even I started to worry: I'd seen the man in the glasses steal a glance at both his cards—he was only pretending that he hadn't seen them. The other three players threw their cards onto the table to show that they were folding. The Mole laid his secret card facedown on the table, covered it with an ashtray, and then removed a wad of notes from his breast pocket and a long thin pay slip. "See this?" he asked his audience, counting the money onto the table. "I've got two thousand *yuan* saved up." He put a thousand on the table. "Fuck it," said the man in glasses. "I'll match you." He counted nine hundred from his wallet, then threw down another thousand. "I'll bet on my own luck. I haven't even looked at my cards. Two thousand!"

The room erupted. "Insane," pronounced the middle-aged goatee who'd opened the door to me. And the Mole's nerve immediately failed him. Staring accusingly at his opponent, he tried to snatch a look at his card: "Swear you haven't seen your hand?" The man in glasses held tightly onto his cards, but the tension was getting to him, too. When he tried to light the cigarette in his mouth, he discovered he was about to burn off the filter and a fair bit of his mouth. "Nervous, are we?" asked the Mole. "I'm betting on my luck," his opponent coolly replied. The Mole recounted his money. The man to his right, one of the players who'd just dropped out, told him he was mad. "Of course he's seen his cards. He's pulled this trick before." "Really?" asked the Mole. "Are you in or not?" interrupted the man in glasses. Mole went on thinking it over. "Because if you're not, you can kiss good-bye to the thousand you just threw in." "Trying to hustle me?" the Mole threw back. The audience began to lose patience: "Are you bastards going to play or not?" someone asked. "We've got to be at work in a few hours. Get a move on." "Stop rushing me," replied the Mole. "Unless you're offering to cover my losses." The man in glasses glanced at his watch. "Forget it," he said serenely, as if already confident of victory. "I've won enough for one evening. Fold." Now Mole properly lost his nerve and declared he was out.

Our champion began raking up his winnings. "That'll buy us all a couple of dinners," muttered an envious onlooker. "Sure," the man in glasses quickly agreed. "Next time we're on nights together." The Mole sat slumped at the table, exhausted by the drama of it. "So what was your card?" he suddenly asked. Pinning it to the table with his elbow, the winner smiled as he totted up his profits: "No play, no see—that's the rule." "Fuck that," said the Mole. "Game's over. Give us a look." His former opponent kept stalling him: "You won't like what you see." "I reckon it was a king," the Mole speculated. With the money stuffed into his wallet, the champion somehow wedged the whole bloated thing into the breast pocket of his uniform. While he was busy with that, the man with the goatee tried to snatch a look at the card, but the winner was too fast for him. "I said, no looking," he repeated, covering it with both hands. "Go on, give us a look," the Goatee wheedled. The victor smugly shook his head again. The Mole threw his own cards onto the table: a decent hand—a pair of tens. Now everyone began shouting at the other man to show his hand. "Fuck it," the winner gave up. "Ten *yuan* and it's yours." Seeing that no one else wanted to volunteer the cash, the Mole threw another ten *yuan* onto the table. "It's your own funeral," the winner said to the Mole as he stuffed the extra money into his pocket. "You can see it, but not until I've left the room. Deal?" Finally taking his hands off the card, he grabbed his lunch box from the windowsill, opened the door, and took off.

The man with the goatee, who was the first to reach the winner's card, carefully turned it over while everyone else crowded behind: it was another jack to match his open card. "No wonder he was so confident," someone said to the Mole. "Just as well you folded." "I knew it," the Mole sighed gnomically. Our visitors gathered their belongings and left, still discussing the game. An old man was the last out of the door: "I can't stop to put the tables back, sorry. I'll be late for work. I'll leave the cards with you for now." My roommates—the only ones left in the room—said that was fine and slowly set about tidying up, still buzzing with the excitement of it. I sat cross-legged on my bed and lit a cigarette. Our resident possessor of a National Basketball Refereeing Qualification (level 3) gathered up the cards and began explaining the rules of a Wuhan game that, he claimed, was much better. He cut the pack with exaggerated expertise; I was sure he wasn't much of a player. "What time is it?" I asked. He suddenly threw down the cards. "Let's have a game. How about it?" "I haven't much money to lose," only one of us objected amid the general murmurs of agreement. "We don't need to bet as much as they did," the basketball referee said. My hemorrhoid-ridden roommate bagged the champion's old seat, insisting it was a lucky chair. As I didn't move anywhere particularly fast, I was left with the Mole's place. Even before we started, everyone had clearly decided I was going to lose.

We began. Since some of us were eager to go to bed, our referee ruled that only losers could drop out. The roommate with hemorrhoids was first to fold. By the time dawn was breaking, there were only two of us left around the table: the basketball referee (on whose nose a new spot had just appeared) and me. The gears in my brain were jammed: I just kept on taking my opponents' money as if I were on autopilot. Soon enough, I was the outright winner. The referee rubbed his teary eyes: "I'm cleaned out." "Want to play on?" I asked him. "I can lend you money." He yawned: "Nah, my luck's off tonight." But he didn't leave the table. I looked out of the window: it was almost light outside. "What time is it?" I asked. "Fuck," the referee said, finally standing up and sliding my winnings over toward him. "I'll count it up for you." Very methodically, he divided the money into its various note values: four hundred *yuan* in total. "You can take this month off," he said enviously. My heart began to pound: "How come?" I replied. He pointed at the money on the table. He watched while I stuffed the money in batches into my pockets and then headed despondently toward the door, where he paused again. I could guess what he was thinking but didn't feel like helping him out. Finally, he asked the question I'd been expecting: "Can you lend us a hundred? You'll get it back next month." I slowly counted it out for him, using the smallest notes I had. "Just give me a hundred note," the referee complained. "If you want it that badly," I told him, "you'll take it as it comes." "I'll pay you back in cents," he told me sourly, as he gathered up the thick, dirty pile of notes (of which the highest denomination was five *yuan*). He slammed the door behind him.

My three roommates were fast asleep. I turned out the light and lay down on my bed. But I immediately felt cold all over and had to sit up again. Miscellaneous footsteps pattered up and down in the corridor outside; people on the early shift were going to the toilet and brushing their teeth. It wouldn't be long, I thought, before everyone would be getting up and I'd be swept along to breakfast and to work. I paced up and down the dorm, feeling that I had to make a decision quickly. "What time is it?" I cried out, hoping that someone would wake up to answer my question. But they all were sleeping like the dead. I opened the door and went to the bathroom. I calmed myself by recounting my money. It wouldn't last forever, I told myself, but it would be enough for now. I splashed my face with cold water, went downstairs, and headed straight for the main entrance to the residential compound.

Its great iron gate was still locked, so I went over to the lit guardhouse. I greeted the janitor, an overweight man with a blue birthmark obscuring at least half his face. He was bent over an aluminum-plated box full of instant noodles, which he was gulping down. "You're up early," he observed. "Off for a run?" "Yes," I quickly agreed. "New, are you?" he asked. "Why d'you ask?" I replied. "Only the new ones have the energy. I'd sleep in if I were you." I smiled back stiffly. To allay his suspicions, I began running as soon as I was out the gate, faster—and faster—and faster.

DA MA'S WAY OF TALKIN
THE MATCHMAKER
THE APPRENTICE

THE FOOTBALL FAN

XIAO LIU
MR. HU, ARE YOU CO
REEDUCATIO
THE WHARF

My name is Chen Zhiqiang. I'm twenty-five years old. I used to work at the Xinhua Printing Factory. My father worked at the same factory all his life. He never smoked a cigarette in his life and then died of lung cancer before he was fifty. No one could understand it.

It was only my father's posthumous influence that got me a job at his old factory as a temporary worker. After five years of this, I was finally installed in a full-time, permanent job in 1992. By then the factory was on the rocks, and it went through several changes of director in quick succession. Though all of them were paid well enough, the factory went on losing money. Then they put a younger man in charge; he started the same year I did. But that's pretty much all we had in common: after all, he had a degree and some ambition. The first thing he did on taking the job was to dish out some massive staff layoffs—everyone made redundant got what boiled down to a retirement package. Have you ever seen someone retired at twenty-five? You're looking at him. My pension's seventy *yuan* a month; I don't think even a cat could live on that.

So everyone went and held a sit-in in front of the municipal government building. Sure, we made a bit of a fuss, but who'd dare push things too far in China in the early 1990s? We just sat there quietly enough; we didn't shout any slogans. It was winter, and our bottoms were almost frostbitten; anyone whose trousers were too thin had to sit in standing up. As the day went on, even people who had on thick trousers had to stand up too. And so the demonstration petered out, without our gaining a single thing from it. After that, the factory's prospects did actually pick up a bit, damn it. So they took pity on us and offered us an extra twenty *yuan* a month as long as we accepted the fact of our retirement without any more fuss. I think that a cat could probably live on ninety *yuan* a month, but it'd be all skin and bones and no good for catching mice.

But I'm losing my train of thought; where was I? Please believe me: I'm not worth your time, I'm just a small-time thief. I'd never do something so horrible. So violent. They say that you get your courage from your gallbladder, right? Well, even if you lent me ten gallbladders, each the size of a football, I wouldn't have been able to do it. I started trembling when I just heard about it; I couldn't stop for two whole days. And even after I stopped, if anyone had just whispered something to me, anything at all, the shaking would start all over again. Sometimes it's just my face trembling like this, but sometimes it's my whole body, like I've just had an electric shock. Something like this can leave me shaking for days, even weeks, shaking so badly I can't even pick up a bowl of rice. My old workmates used to think I was always ill, that I had malaria. In fact, I'm just anxious. Actually, it wasn't exactly that. Like sometimes I'd spend a whole day at home, all the doors and windows locked, or sunning myself in the square near the Drum Tower, where no one knows me. And I'd still be shaking. What did I have to be worried about there? In truth, I wasn't really anxious, but I still couldn't stop myself trembling. Afterward I gradually got used to it, I got used to spending whole days shaking like a leaf. It was a very strange feeling. When no one was around, I could even start to enjoy it: it was oddly comforting. It got so that if I suddenly stopped trembling, I would get even more anxious—I can't explain it.

I'm sorry. I seem to have wandered off the subject again. As I was saying, I'm not worth bothering with. I'm just a small-time thief. The most expensive thing I've ever stolen was an almost-new second-hand bike with twenty-six-inch wheels, and that was a good few years ago. I'd found the bike at the bottom of the apartment building and carried it up the stairs in the middle of the night. It had a cane seat on the back. I spent the rest of the night smashing the lock with a hammer covered in tape. And I was too useless even to manage that. It was dawn before I got the job done. What? Why did I cover the hammer in tape? I didn't want to wake my mother; she was asleep in the room next door. As it got light outside, I started to worry that she would wake up any moment; since my father died, she's started getting up early. What would she think if she saw the bike? So I decided to take it back to where I'd found it, this time without its lock. When I got down to the third floor, someone called out to me from somewhere above. I looked up and saw it was the young man who lived above us: he was wearing red running clothes with white trim. He seemed full of energy, full of high spirits. Why did it have to turn out to be *his* bike? You can probably work out what happened after that. Does that really count as a criminal record? I'm just a bit of a weak character; I've slipped into a few bad habits. That's all. Believe me: I'd never do anything so horrible. I can't stand the sight of blood.

*

My name is Chen Zhiqiang. I'm twenty-five years old. I used to work at the Xinhua Printing Factory. My father worked at the same factory all his life. He'd never smoked a cigarette in his life and then died of lung cancer before he was fifty. No one could understand it.

The funny thing about my father is that he never once went to hospital until the end. He was an unremarkable man in most ways, but at least he stayed healthy most of his life; and nothing particularly bad—no serious illness or personal misfortune—ever happened to him. Well, not until the illness that killed him, anyway. When the government started reforming our industries, the printing plant introduced a new system for health insurance: the factory gave employees twenty *yuan* a month per person for medical costs. Anything beyond that first twenty *yuan*, the factory only paid 20 percent—the rest had to be covered by the individual in question. Every month, my father took that extra twenty *yuan* back to my mother; he was the envy of all his colleagues. I remember him being pretty delighted with himself about it. Every month he was obsessed with pocketing every cent of that twenty *yuan*.

Eventually, though, he just had to go to hospital to find out what was wrong with him. It was the first time he'd been in his life. The doctors told him to make his funeral arrangements. He fainted on the spot. I remember Father when he was close to death: I remember his chewing on a bone, like a dog, an almost savage glare in his eyes. I felt somehow as if he were chewing on that twenty *yuan* that he'd saved every month all those years on medical fees.

Let's change the subject. But I often find myself talking to other people about my father, particularly when I'm trembling about something. It's strange, but when I talk about him I don't tremble so badly. What did you say that old lady's name was? Mrs. Wu. I never even met her. I didn't even know she lived in our building until after the incident. She was a strange one. I didn't know what staircase or floor she lived on. How old was she? Sixty-eight? Heavens, what a terrible way for a sixty-eight-year-old woman to die. That's horrible. I'd heard that she was very rich and that she dressed very young, very fashionably, for her age. She didn't like to admit she was getting old. Even though she'd lost her figure and was covered in wrinkles, she wasn't shy about showing herself off. My neighbors all said she was asking for trouble. Women are like clams; their shells should be shut tight. If you're always opening yourself out, sooner or later someone or something will slip inside. I'm just reporting what people said after she died. I don't even remember what she looked like. I'd never seen her, so of course I couldn't remember what she looked like.

We've been talking for ages now. Surely you don't believe that I did it? Your imagination's running away with you. How could I dream of doing something like that to a sixty-eight-year-old woman? She was five years older than my own mother. Even if I were running a high fever, 106 or 107 degrees, I'd never dream of doing anything like that.

Oh, I remember now: I might have seen Mrs. Wu once. One evening when my mother and I were coming back from buying food at the market, we bumped into a woman in a cheongsam coming down the middle staircase of our block. I got the sense that she and my mother had known each other a long time, though not particularly well. In fact, I picked up on a slightly strange dynamic between them. They stood there a while, chatting politely about nothing in particular. I stood by, excluded from the conversation, holding the basket of food. I remember that the woman gave off a very curious kind of perfume. My mother, you see, never smelled of anything at all; she had no more scent than a shadow. Without anything to go on, I got the confused idea that my silent father was somehow behind the strange way the two women were behaving toward each other. As I say, it was a random idea, but there was also a touch of inspiration about it. I remember that after they'd finished talking, the woman stroked my head. Yes, it's all coming back to me: that woman in a sky-blue, shiny silk cheongsam, slit to the waist, bending down to rub my head. I was still very small then, only this high. I was probably only five at the time. As she squatted down, the evening sun was behind her head, casting her face into darkness, so I couldn't make out her features properly. That must have been twenty years ago, or more. And even now I wouldn't swear that the woman in the cheongsam was the Mrs. Wu who met such an unfortunate end twenty years later. I just couldn't be sure.

*

My name is Chen Zhiqiang. I'm twenty-five years old. I used to work at the Xinhua Printing Factory. My father worked at the same factory all his life. He'd never smoked a cigarette in his life and then died of lung cancer before he was fifty. No one could understand it.

Until the last few years that I was at the printing workshop, my colleagues would sometimes speak respectfully about my father because he had spent so many decades around the factory's rows of clanking old machinery; every spare part had his workmanship on it. Please don't interrupt: if you want to understand me, we have to go back to my father. I'm trembling, can't you see? It's worst inside my head. I have to calm myself down before I can tell you anything useful.

But in my last years at the factory, no one wanted to talk about my father, for a simple reason: the factory had been extended and all the old machinery replaced. I think the ghost of my father often hangs around the factory workshop, watching the action; he would be delighted by how much bigger the place is now. The only drawback is that people can no longer say hello to him, and he can't say hello to them. My father loved his work, you see. There was nothing particularly technically skilled about what he did; anyone could have done it. It was low-grade, dirty physical labor—completely mechanical. So I felt that it didn't really matter whether or not I wanted to take over from my father: it was just something that I had to go and keep doing. But now I'm retired, too. I think my father would have been a lot more upset about it than I was. And I can see exactly why they retired me at twenty-five. From my very first day in the printing workshop, I knew that I wasn't me—I was my father. My father had borrowed my body so that he could keep working from beyond the grave—even though he'd reached retirement age. Even though he deserved a rest; he never got one when he was alive.

Sorry, I'm feeling better now; I'll do my best to answer your questions. Since retiring, I've spent most of my time at home. I hardly ever go out; I know almost nothing about what's going on outside our apartment. I didn't see anyone suspicious that day. Or let me put it another way: before the incident, I never gave anyone a second thought, but now I find everyone suspicious. Have you talked to those door-to-door peddlers, the ones from out of town? Or insurance salesmen? There are so many people like that around these days—as many as the cigarette butts you see scattered all over the pavement. It's the ones selling kitchen knives who I think are the dodgiest characters. Say Mrs. Wu didn't want to buy one of his knives, so he hacked her to death. I bet that's what happened, you know. What? She was strangled with a rope? Well, you should go and find someone who sells nylon rope, then. Why are you bothering with me?

Please don't hit me. Please. Please. All right, here's another possibility. Probably about a week ago, a stray dog turned up at the base of our apartment block. It was yellowish and skinny, and its stomach seemed to be glued flat to its spine. Its back was covered in bald patches, and it had an open, festering wound on its rear, full of maggots. You could see its thing, swinging from side to side, covered in dirt. So it was a male dog; that's an important detail. For a few days, the dog hung around at the bottom of our staircase, but after the incident, it disappeared completely. Suspicious, wouldn't you say? I didn't tell you this earlier because—well, it's awkward. One day, coming back from buying the newspaper, I saw it scrabbling about by the rubbish bin. I whistled at it. It slowly turned to face me. It had a bone in its mouth, and its eyes—they had a sadness in them, a sense of grievance. I recognized that look immediately. It was my father, back from the dead; I knew it. Though I don't know what he'd come back for. All day, I felt oppressed by the encounter: my father had been dead all these years, and I still couldn't understand him. I'm sure that the dog raped old Mrs. Wu, 100 percent. You should go and arrest it, right now, but please don't tell anyone I gave you the tip-off. My father was disappointed enough with me while he was alive; I don't want him to feel the same in the underworld.

✶

My name is Chen Zhiqiang. I'm twenty-five years old. I used to work at the Xinhua Printing Factory. My father worked at the same factory all his life. He'd never smoked a cigarette in his life and then died of lung cancer before he was fifty. No one could understand it.

My mother can't understand why you've arrested me, either. She's tried everything to find me a girlfriend: she's asked all sorts of people to help—aunts and uncles, grandparents, from both sides of the family. She's dragged over just about every girl in the city that she had any connection with at all and exhibited them all before me, like a magic lantern show. But I wasn't interested in any of them. Luckily for my mother, I was utterly scrupulous in how I treated them, too—or else she would have been little better than a pimp. You could have arrested *her* and put her away for twelve years. You'd laugh at the things my mother's done. Every girl she invited she slipped a small, stiff red package: money for the taxi ride to our apartment and back. Normally, she walked everywhere or, at best, took the bus; even a minibus was too luxurious for my mother. I remember the last girl she had over, last week it would have been: she was slim but well endowed and with her own apartment, too. My mother stood by hopefully, looking like she might faint at any moment at this golden opportunity. But I couldn't look her in the eye. Even though I knew that my mother was almost speechless with excitement at the prospect of this girl, I refused her without any hesitation. My mother took my decision calmly enough, but her hair went completely white afterward. Logically speaking, I had no right to be choosy; I'm not exactly a catch. But I have a problem when it comes to marriage, a big problem. I'll be frank with you: I'm homosexual. By which I mean that I've never slept with a woman, not even once. Right now, I've got dozens of boyfriends: different classes, different jobs, different sorts, but they'll all testify to my good character. Please, no violence, I'm begging you, I'm begging you. Don't hit me. Actually, I'm enjoying this. My favorite boyfriend, a grade 3 cook in the cafeteria in the provincial party committee offices; he's just like this with me every time we meet; he's never easy on me. I feel almost blessed. Don't hit me.

Don't hit me. Don't hit me. Don't hit me. Don't hit me. Don't hit me. Don't hit me. Don't hit me. Don't hit me.

All right, I'll be straight with you. My father's still the problem. Even though he left us years ago, I haven't had a moment's peace since his death. Though he lived with my mother for decades, he didn't love her. They were like two colleagues who just happened to live together and who'd run out of things to say to each other. For decades my father was secretly in love with someone else: Mrs. Wu, who'd been widowed all those years ago. My father really was a proper person, someone who followed the rules, who never overstepped boundaries, so all he could do was bury his passion deep inside. Eventually, and not surprisingly, the strain killed him. But there's a twist to the story. That afternoon, my father's ghost—tortured with regret—possessed me to climb up the stairwell and knock on Mrs. Wu's door. As soon as she opened the door, she knew what I'd come for and burst into tears. After the two of them had completed their business, Mrs. Wu lay stunned on the bed, before suddenly springing up to grab hold of my leg. She begged my father to take her away, forever. To bring to an end to the waiting that should have ended so long ago. After thinking it over, my father went to the cupboard and took out some nylon cord.

✶

My name is Chen Zhiqiang. I'm twenty-five years old. I used to work at the Xinhua Printing Factory. My father worked at the same factory all his life. He'd never smoked a cigarette in his life and then died of lung cancer before he was fifty. No one could understand it.

I think I've worked out what happened now. Maybe you follow the same methods as doctors: maybe you trust only evidence like urine, hair, or fingerprints and then conclude that someone's got an incurable disease or has committed a crime. But life's not as simple as that. You must have some cast-iron proof about me; well, draw your own conclusions then. I admit everything; will that do? Can I go to sleep now? Just for a little while, I beg you. I really am so tired. Just let me close my eyes for a little, will you? Just five minutes. How about it? I'm begging you. Or could I have a sip of water? Just a sip. My throat's so dry it feels like there's smoke coming off it. I've already swallowed all my saliva, all my phlegm. I'm begging you. There are so many of you, you can take turns. But there's only one of me; it's not fair. Where's my father now? Why isn't he here to share the blame? I bet he and Mrs. Wu are lying somewhere together, gabbing away about the ineffable sadness of separation. They're happy while I'm suffering. Are you going to let me go to the toilet? I haven't been for two days. My bladder hurts so much I can't even feel it anymore. I can't even sit up straight. I'm begging you. I'm going to piss on myself. Oh, well. Don't mind the smell. That's better, so much better. Look, if I confess, will you let me sleep? All right. You've won. I'll tell you everything. In truth, I never planned to hide anything from you. You know, people who have committed crimes always want to be punished for them; they're just too weak to tell anyone what they've done. I understand that even death's too good for me after what I've done, but I still find it hard to talk about.

All right, if we're going to begin at the beginning, we should start with Diego Maradona. Surely you've heard of Maradona? The greatest football genius the world has ever seen? If you haven't heard of him, I think you're even worse than I am. Please, no violence, I'm begging you. Anyway, you're wasting your energy by hitting me because everything I'm telling you now is the truth. Can I go on now? Can I? All right. I'm a fully paid-up football fanatic. I've never met anyone as mad about football as I am. I used to play a bit when I was younger, at sports school, but I've never watched the Chinese professional league matches, neither live nor on television. Do you know why? Do you know why the government began developing a professional football league after 1990? Well, I'll tell you: it's a conspiracy, that's what. They wanted everyone to vent their feelings in the football stands, to distract them from all their old grievances, to make them forget what had happened the year before. I wasn't having any of it; I didn't want to go along with their rotten conspiracy. Go to any stadium in the country and you'll see what I mean: all those crowds of overexcited fans, waving their arms and screaming hysterically, shouting obscenities. They're not really screaming about football, you know.

Sorry. Sorry. I seem to have wandered off the subject again. Although I don't watch the league, I do follow football news. Six months ago, I read in the newspaper that Maradona was going to visit China with the Boca Juniors. I literally fainted with excitement. After I came around, I took another look at the newspaper. It really was true: there was going to be a match at the stadium at Mount Wutai; I fainted again. There was no one I worshipped more than Maradona; I thought he was the most gifted individual to be born on this planet since World War II. OK, you don't agree with me. No great surprise there. These days, no one talks that much about Maradona anymore, I know. Or people think he's just a clown or a buffoon. But when it comes down to it, who isn't? Anyway, the world has always been tough on geniuses. To begin with, I refused to believe what the newspapers were telling me. Until Mount Wutai Stadium started advertising advance sales for this one-off friendly. That's when I stopped doubting the news. The feet of the great Maradona were really going to trample the bald pitch of Mount Wutai Stadium; the whole idea of it was more thrilling to me than a sighting of Halley's Comet. That day, I stayed in bed, weeping hot tears. I wanted something very simple: to see Maradona for myself while I was still young. Even if I were miles off in the stands, it would be enough for me. But the tickets were too expensive and I was too broke; I just couldn't afford a hundred-*yuan* ticket. You're taking this all down in evidence, I suppose? So in the end I had to sell my blood to boost my funds. I put the ticket inside a picture frame and hung it on the wall opposite my bed. Every day I would stare at it till I was dizzy with concentration, counting down the days. I expect you know what happened next: for unknown reasons, the friendly match was canceled. Mount Wutai Stadium put out another advertisement, apologizing and asking those who had already bought tickets to come and pick up a refund. But I kept the ticket—it's still hanging on my wall. Now I think back on it, it was that moment that poisoned me, that lodged in me a violent hatred toward the world. Even if I didn't feel it at the time. A few days ago, I happened to see Maradona again on the television: he was fat, completely out of shape. He was sitting in the stands watching a Boca Juniors match, looking utterly dejected. The Boca Juniors were having a terrible season, with no prospect of its getting any better. I still don't know what it was exactly that overcame me, but for some reason, my anger got the better of me. I lost my head. Maybe you should get an expert to do some tests on me. Maybe I'm schizophrenic. So I can't remember exactly what happened next—luckily, you seem to have a pretty clear sense of the sequence of events. I'll pay for what I did; that's only right and proper. My only regret is that I never will see Maradona for myself now.

✶

My name is Chen Zhiqiang. I'm twenty-five years old. I used to work at the Xinhua Printing Factory. My father worked at the same factory all his life. He'd never smoked a cigarette in his life and then died of lung cancer before he was fifty. No one could understand it.

Go on, hit me some more—beat me to death. Why are you suddenly being so nice to me? You're confusing me. Oh, I get it. You think I'm good as dead already, don't you? I feel so relaxed all of a sudden. I don't know why. Maybe I think I've already died, too. Everything has a span: people have a lifetime, plants a season. All right then, speaking as a dead man, I'm going to tell you exactly what happened. I've exhausted myself with all these stories. Can you imagine how exhausted a dead man feels?

I already told you that I was completely broke—you should have filed that important piece of evidence away somewhere. So that much was true. I also told you that I'm a small-time thief. Remember that, too? You'd have to cut the hands of a thief off before he'd resort to selling his blood. So of course, someone like me was sure that I could find another solution to my cash-flow problem; I'd find the hundred *yuan* from somewhere else. One afternoon, I had been loitering around the middle staircase in our block. It was very quiet: everyone was at work. No one else had the luck to have retired at twenty-five. I didn't have a big heist in mind; I planned only to rummage through the random objects piled outside each door, to pocket a couple of things that might be useful for generating a bit of spare cash. A pair of leather shoes, maybe; they might cover half a football ticket. If they were designer, they'd probably easily stretch to two tickets. When I got to the sixth floor, I noticed that the door wasn't latched. My heart suddenly began to pound: although I'd been pilfering stuff for years, I'd never dared set foot in someone else's house. This was something new. I waited for ages outside the door, listening for a sign of life inside. Eventually, I plucked up the courage to go in. The sitting room was in darkness; everything was very neat, but there seemed to be a layer of dust on the table. After knocking several times on the door without getting any response, I slipped inside and carefully closed the door behind me. Even if the room were full of banknotes, I said to myself, I'd take only a hundred, or maybe two fifties—and it was all Maradona's fault, anyway. But when I took my search to the back bedroom, I suddenly froze. An old lady, half lying across the bed, was looking sedately at me. "You're—you're at home," I stammered. "That's right," came the reply. What was I to do next? After a long pause, I clenched my trembling fists. "Give me all your money!" I shouted. But even as I made my decision, I felt only despair: I knew that all was lost. Mrs. Wu stayed very calm: she kept her money in a pocket in her underwear, she told me. If I wanted it, I had to come and get it myself. I approached her nervously. While I was extracting the single fifty-*yuan* note, my fingers brushed against her warm body. That's when things took an unexpected turn. I admit that I went mad, but I swear I didn't use violence; in truth, I was trembling too much to be of any use. If she hadn't helped me, her hot legs twisted tightly around me, I would never have got the thing done. Badly shaken, I stumbled and fell down the staircase as I tried to leave. When I got up again, I had the overwhelming sense of having fallen into a trap. I wondered if Mrs. Wu had been leaving her door open for years. After this thought occurred to me, I even began to feel that I had done something noble—an act of charity. Of course, this feeling didn't last. From that time on, whenever I needed fifty *yuan*, I would go up to the sixth floor. Every time, she would have only fifty *yuan* for me. She was always very clear, very firm, about this. If I wanted a hundred *yuan*, I'd have to make two visits. I became sick with myself. After it had been going on for a few months, I could bear it no longer; I hated myself too much. I told myself that I was a useless bastard, that I deserved to die if I went again. And you know, I really did give her up. Although I couldn't forget what I'd done, I couldn't forget those strange, dreamlike encounters; I still hoped the memory would fade with time. But three days ago, late at night, Mrs. Wu suddenly appeared from out of the shadows when I was at the bottom of our staircase and pushed me toward the bicycle shed. "Listen," she hissed, her hair disheveled. "I'm going to tell the police." "Tell them what?" I asked. "What do you think?" she replied. "So what are you going to do about it?"

And that's all I'm going to tell you. Look, I'm trembling again. What have I got left to tremble about? But I've finally worked out why I'm shaking. It's because I'm afraid.

DA MA'S WAY OF TALKI
THE MATCHMAKER
THE APPRENTICE
THE FOOTBALL FA

XIAO LIU

MR. HU, ARE YOU COM
REEDUCATIO
THE WHARF

Allow me to introduce my friend Xiao Liu.* His real name is Liu Guixiang, and he'll be fifty this year. He was born in the year of the ox, which makes him a whole lunar cycle and a half older than me, and he works in the IT department of the Soil Research Institute here in Nanjing. He received some semblance of a further education at the end of the Cultural Revolution, spending two years at the Nanjing Workers' College (now Southeast University) in the Department of Mechanical Engineering, after which he was assigned by our wonderful state planners to the Soil Research Institute (to a job that had, naturally, not a blessed thing to do with anything he had previous studied). His lack of a proper degree had bothered him ever since Mao and

* The "Xiao" adds an affectionate diminutive to his surname, Liu.

his mischief-making educational policies came to an end, until finally in 1988 he managed to get a BA through a correspondence course. That year, he also turned thirty-nine and joined the party. He told me at the time (and I recall several other forty-something friends saying something similar, so let it count as a representative symptom of midlife crisis) that he'd been doing some long-term thinking recently: he still had hopes of getting a job in local government and a slightly bigger apartment.

Unfortunately, a string of distracting misfortunes came his way. First his six-year-old son, Liu Gang, got tubercular meningitis, then his elderly father died, then his younger sister got her leg crushed in a motorcycle accident and had to come to Nanjing for an operation. Finally, at the end of that annus horribilis, he separated from his wife, Lin Zhimin, a local Nanjinger and an accountant in the Irrigation Research Bureau. Three years later they divorced, with the court giving him custody of their son. Xiao Liu explained the causes of the rupture in only the sketchiest terms. The two of them had never gotten along particularly well, he told me; they were always arguing about one thing or another. At the end of each of their regular fights, she'd fling some clothes into a bag and retreat to her parents' place for a couple of weeks. I'm sure that Xiao Liu sometimes deliberately provoked arguments just to get some relief. So the news of their breakup wasn't a shock; what surprised me was that Xiao Liu had the resolve to get a divorce. Of course, it turned out that it was Lin Zhimin who pushed it through. As soon as things loosened up a bit after Mao's death, she found herself a lover, though Xiao Liu didn't discover this (and in his own marital bed, too) until deep into the 1980s.

It was a little before this that he'd discovered why the water kept cutting out on the top floors of his apartment building. He'd just been transferred to the housing department in the Soil Research Institute, and his department head had put him in charge of improving the older buildings in the residential compounds. He'd been obsessed with radios since high school; he lived and breathed multimeters, soldering irons, and diodes, and he had a decent, hands-on understanding of how they worked. After a little jiggery-pokery and the addition of a pressure pump, he came up with a device that meant that the inhabitants of the fourth floor and above never needed to worry again about the water supply. This represented, I understood, the pinnacle of Xiao Liu's engineering career, although he later had a minor stroke of genius over television circuits, apparently improving their efficiency by 70 percent. Once confirmed by a succession of relevant experts, his innovation was included in that year's Provincial Plan for Strategic Technology. Although he later seemed rather embarrassed by this success, at the time his invention improved his life in a number of ways. The senior management initially remained oblivious to its potential, probably because neither they nor any of their relatives lived above the third floor. But news of the contraption spread like wildfire, and several households from the upper stories asked Xiao Liu to come and fix their water supply problems. Xiao Liu charged a hundred *yuan*—including labor and materials—for each pressure pump that he fitted, meaning that he made more than fifty *yuan* on each device. Each staircase with this problem needed one of his pressure pumps, and each department in the institute had several dodgy old buildings.

Soon Xiao Liu needed an assistant, which is where I came into the picture. We'd work nights together, assembling the parts. I wasn't capable of much more than the finishings, but it was all fiddly, manual work. So I suggested that he raise the price, to 150 *yuan* apiece. Xiao Liu hit his forehead: "Of course—why didn't I think of that?" They still sold like hot cakes, even at the new price; so we raised it again, to 200. At this, he became a little uneasy; "What next?" he asked me, "250?" When Xiao Liu's department head got wind of Xiao Liu's second stream of income, he was furious until he got a better idea. He detailed two employees to help Xiao Liu with installation and negotiated a cut for the department. Even though the department was now creaming off most of the profit, Xiao Liu felt he was doing well enough from it—maybe he was making a bit less than before, but he felt more comfortable about it. And he got to use the departmental tools and workshop space.

The head of housing was considerably savvier than Xiao Liu—he quickly realized this was worth getting a patent for. (Up to this point, Xiao Liu had simply been smearing the circuit boards and internal parts of all the installed pumps with black ink to keep his trade secret from others.) But as soon as Xiao Liu went to consult the new provincial patents bureau, he got cold feet: he discovered that applying for them cost money, around two thousand *yuan*. At this moment, his head of department generously decided to advance the money himself and the patent was quickly approved, granted jointly to Xiao Liu and the Soil Research Institute Housing Department. (Xiao Liu was not particularly delighted about this: what had the housing department ever invented?) Seized by the entrepreneurial spirit then sweeping the country, the head of housing applied for an institute loan to start a factory to produce the pumps on an industrial scale, and Xiao Liu stopped grumbling after he was promoted to the rank of midlevel technician. The senior management at the Soil Research Institute—which was one big financial black hole—was naturally delighted at the prospect of a moneymaking opportunity. But as soon as preparations were under way, the management encountered a problem that on the surface was a disagreement about naming the product but in reality went far deeper—Xiao Liu's head of department had been avoiding the subject of how much of the profits from this new venture were to go to the inventor. Anyway, Xiao Liu wanted the pump named after him. The head of department countered that such an idea was vulgar individualism. The director of the institute finally intervened by choosing the "Good Earth," which contained a highly pertinent reference to soil while sounding auspiciously expansive. Although Xiao Liu wasn't particularly happy, there wasn't much he could do about it.

Just when the loan had been approved, a new product burst onto the market, the King of Faucets, which shared many similarities with the Good Earth while managing to be considerably cheaper. What Facebook was to the Winklevoss twins, the King of Faucets was to Xiao Liu. The head of department bought one and asked Xiao Liu to check it out; he was sure their design had been ripped off and was totally ready to sue. Three months of frenetic litigation later, the Good Earth Pressure Pump factory closed before it had even opened. The King of Faucets management produced a wad of documentation proving that their product had been patented before the Good Earth. They warned the

Soil Institute that if they went ahead manufacturing their Good Earth Pressure Pump, they'd sue *their* asses for infringement of copyright. While all this was going on, the King of Faucets even managed to bring out an improved, second-generation model. When the National Patent Office told Xiao Liu that it was thinking of canceling his certificate, Xiao Liu dropped the whole thing; if he lost the patent, would he lose his promotion too? Was the King of Faucets going to sue him for all the pumps he'd already installed? His love affair with radio technology crumbled to dust and nothingness. In all the years he'd been messing around with radios, all he'd managed to invent was something someone else had already thought of. He promptly switched his allegiance to computers.

So the head of housing's get-rich-quick scheme was aborted. He tore his copy of the patent certificate in two, threw it in the bin, and settled down to wait quietly for retirement. He had several powerful analogies for the new socioeconomic phenomenon of patents, Xiao Liu—who took this setback much better than his boss—told me. "You see a woman walking along the street," he'd counseled Xiao Liu when he was originally getting him to apply. "Even if no one else has seen her, she isn't yours yet. So you smear ink all over her face—but other men can still smell her. Hide her in a hole underground, and she's still no use to you because she's not yours yet. Stand guard over her with a gun and you're still not safe—the moment you go off for a piss, she'll run off with someone else. That's why you have to get a marriage license. That way, she's yours. A patent's just like that: it means other men can only look, not touch. And you have to act fast because there are lots of other men out there with eyes in their heads. Get it?" *After* the litigation debacle, the head of housing's logic took on a more melancholic tone: "You see a woman walking down the street; anyone can look at her, but only the first person to see her can have her. A patent's just like that. Get it?" Xiao Liu would later come to feel that his head of department's sage similes had laid the imaginative groundwork for his own divorce, which he took much more easily as a result.

I was only seventeen when Xiao Liu dragged me into his business venture. I'd just started college in Nanjing—at Southeast University, his own alma mater, but in a different department (power engineering). It was because of Xiao Liu that I'd ended up at a Nanjing college rather than in Beijing, which I'd set my sights on going to. I'll have more to say about that later. Every time I helped with his business venture, however little I did, Xiao Liu insisted on giving me twenty *yuan*. To begin with, he'd wanted to pay me thirty, but I managed to haggle him down. And so it was that after doing almost nothing at all, I had four hundred *yuan* to my name. My parents wired me forty *yuan* a month for living expenses, so I'd basically got my hands on a whole year's allowance without even thinking about it. As soon as the New Year holiday arrived, I bought a ticket to Harbin, the frozen city beyond the Great Wall. For one, I had a classmate from Harbin, called Zhang Dong, and we got along pretty well. Second, I'd always liked the name Harbin—it sounded exotically remote. When I looked it up in the dictionary, I discovered it was a transliteration into Chinese characters of Russian words meaning "Where Fishing Nets Dry."

It did not occur to me even once that a place where you dried fishing nets could also be cold. After the train had passed Shanhaiguan, the easternmost fort in the Great Wall, the desolation of the scenery outside the window forced me to make a realistic projection about Harbin's probable temperature (the train itself was seriously over-centrally heated; it gave me a bad headache, but at least it wasn't cold). As the train moved through the landscape, my forecasts steadily fell. Even so, the coldness exceeded my most extravagant expectations. My first thought on leaving the station was to wonder why on earth I wasn't wearing more clothes.

Zhang Dong's family lived in a suburban slum of single-story houses: the nine of them were crammed into less than 215 square feet. They had no central heating, of course: the only warmth inside the house came from pipes that ran from the stove into the hollow partition walls. My arrival only increased the intense pressure on space and resources in their household. And yet they were irrepressibly hospitable, and the more welcoming they were, the worse I felt. The interior of the house was divided into several small rooms, with the largest given over to Zhang Dong's parents. His father was a retired worker, probably somewhere in his sixties—a patriarch with a savage temper. Every evening, he'd settle down with a flask of warm wine, roaring at his family between sips. It was Zhang Dong's mother who generally got the worst of it. Everywhere they went, Zhang Dong's two married older brothers brought with them beaten-tin lunch boxes filled with tobacco. They were as brutal to their wives as their father was to their mother; they spoke only to shout at them. Perhaps Zhang Dong's second brother shouted a little less, partly because he liked to hit his wife, too. She spent most of her time by the stove making dumplings, the tears rolling down her bruised face. It was a perfect revelation to me: I had no idea that men could be such emperors in their own house.

Zhang Dong, my classmate, was a late third son and the first of the family to get into university. Though he never had a lot to say for himself, he was made much of, so the largest bed in the house was cleared for him and me to sleep on. My first few days there, Zhang Dong took me around the city after breakfast. Because all the clothes I'd brought were too thin for the Harbin winter, I had to borrow a heavy blue wadded-cotton overcoat belonging to Zhang Dong's father and a shabby fur hat belonging to Zhang Dong's oldest brother. The coat was ripped at the armpit seam, and every few steps I had to pause to stuff the sallow wadding back inside. We'd wander about the city until it got dark, have dinner, and then go out again to Zhaolin Park where the annual ice and snow festival was on—the park was filled with frozen monuments (mainly animals or buildings) carved by sculptors from all over the world. By the time we got back, Zhang Dong's family were asleep. Though I got the feeling that Zhang Dong didn't want to spend more time at home than he had to, he didn't seem to want to tell me about it either. Within a couple of days, we'd walked just about everywhere there was to walk: along the Slavonic apartment blocks lining Central Avenue, around Stalin Park and the snow sculptures of Sun Island. I'd also discovered that Harbin's north wind was more than capable of freezing your eyeballs into immobility. I began to wonder if Zhang Dong had packed my schedule this tightly so that I could get my sightseeing done and go home as soon as possible. Maybe he'd extended his invitation to me only casually; maybe he'd never thought I'd be tactless enough to take him up on it. There was no way I could stay until the New Year—it was a long ten days away. But when I suggested I go home, Zhang Dong and his family fiercely fought the idea. How could I think of coming all this way and not staying for New Year? The worry lines across his mother's forehead visibly deepened: did I think they were too poor to give me anything decent to eat? Was the bed too uncomfortable? I immediately retracted the idea, mortified at their suspicions. I was warmed by the generosity and directness of people from the north of my country and irritated by my own convoluted, second-guessing southern instincts.

We couldn't go out for the next few days after that. The ground-level temperature was so low that the pavements had completely frozen over. And Zhang Dong's family wanted to keep him at home a little more, to enjoy the short, precious holiday time. I tried as hard as I could to reinvent myself as a member of Zhang Dong's family: to enjoy the daily, banal pleasures of life in their home; to appreciate the great good fortune of being able to sit inside, watching the New Year's snow swirl outside the windows. At meal times, I gulped down vast quantities of pickled cabbage—a substance I usually shunned—to demonstrate my dedication to the vegetable that dominated their diet. After a few days, I discovered to my surprise, I had taken to it. I could not get the hang of their toilets, though. As there was no bathroom in the house, they and their neighbors had to use a semiexposed communal pit latrine. The inside of the toilet alone—scattered with rods of excrement and icicles of urine—gave me pause. The winter had frozen everything solid—even the smell had been neutralized by the subzero temperatures. The pit itself—on which you needed to squat—was carpeted by glistening ice; I was terrified that I would slip on it. You had only a moment to complete your business before severe frostbite kicked in. When I failed to seize this moment several days in a row, Zhang Dong took me to a toilet in a children's hospital nearby (one stop on the bus) that was—luxury—centrally heated. A streetcar stop was located by the main entrance, and every morning as I emerged from the hospital at rush hour, a crowd of people were waiting beneath the sign, snorting white vapor, stamping their feet. I enjoyed standing there, watching. The faces of Harbin women had larger pores than those of their southern counterparts, and they wore far more foundation; their skin always had a greenish-white tinge to it—I liked it, it made them seem more solid, more real, somehow. The men, by contrast, seemed dull, depressed, enveloped in the smell of tobacco. As I contemplated them, I realized that this breed of woman was forever condemned to this breed of man: they cooked for them, they had their children, they were beaten by them. What must they think of it all?

One figure in particular drew my attention. She was tall—around five feet six—and straight backed; she wore a hip-length red down jacket, her long, slender legs ending in a pair of black riding boots. A black braid hung down her back, and her neck was muffled in a white scarf. When the streetcar arrived, everyone rushed to the doors—except for her. She waited patiently at the back of the crowd. After the streetcar had left, she stood at the front of those left behind; she glanced in the direction in which the streetcar had come and then looked back out over the street. Because she turned away so fast, I didn't get a look at her face, though for some reason I got the idea she had very long eyelashes. By this point, Zhang Dong was starting to complain at the cold and wanted to hurry on home; I asked him to let me stay a little longer. But she didn't turn back around. I began to think perhaps it would be best if I didn't see her face; she was so alluring from behind, it would be crushingly disappointing if her face turned out to be ordinary, or even unattractive. For that, surely, is the way things always do turn out. The moment I had formulated my theory, she turned around as if to refute it: her eyes were a clear, brilliant blue, slightly sunken, and colder than the January wind that was gusting around us. My throat tightened; the blood surged through me. Though she was looking in my direction, there was something empty in those piercing eyes; I could find no reflection of myself, no acknowledgment of my existence. Before I had gotten a proper look at her face, I had to look away, down at my feet, my face blazing scarlet as if she had seen into my soul. I had only a vague, imperfect sense of her features. I yearned to stand alongside her—a couple of steps was all it would have taken—and survey her at my leisure. An instant later, though, I remembered what I was wearing: the matted hat, the ancient coat. My courage deserted me: I felt I could not bear to be noticed by that aquamarine stare, not in my current state. But at the same time I craved another look at her. I stood there, paralyzed by indecision, allowing my resolve to ebb away quietly. When the streetcar finally carried her off, ringing its bell, I sighed, almost in relief. I remembered Zhang Dong. He had already set off for home but had paused a little way ahead to wait for me, his neck shrunk into his shoulders, his mittened hands shielding his nose. He motioned with his head to indicate that I should catch up.

Zhang Dong didn't seem too fazed by my performance at the streetcar stop; as we walked along, he explained briefly that she was an *ermao*. When I failed to understand the local argot, he enlarged a little. Before the Russian Revolution, a great many refugees had fled to Harbin and settled there. Several generations later, they were completely naturalized; the only thing that distinguished them from the locals was their physiology. Purebred Russians were called *lao maozi*—literally, "old hairy ones." But Eurasians, those with mixed Russian and Chinese blood, were called *ermao*, "second hairy ones." I asked him if all half Russians were as beautiful as she was. Some are pig ugly, Zhang Dong replied. Despite the contempt in his voice, I immediately thought of my favorite Russian literary heroines: Anna Karenina, Tonia from *How the Steel Was Tempered*, or Chekhov's heroine in "Anna on the Neck." My heart began to beat faster as I nursed the memory of those blue eyes. But I dropped the subject; I didn't want Zhang Dong to think me naive.

The next day when I went to the toilet, I didn't wear the coat or the fur hat. Zhang Dong's mother told me I couldn't go out like that, that I'd freeze to death. I didn't mind, I replied, it wasn't far and I was going to run—I needed the exercise. Zhang Dong's face twisted with displeasure; I suspected that he'd realized I didn't want to wear his family's old clothes outside. But my mind was on other things. He sourly told me I shouldn't be running in this weather, that the air would destroy my lungs, and he left it at that. It wasn't as bad as he'd said it would be: although my nose ran with the cold, I felt much better for the brisk run. If I saw my half Russian again, I was determined to get a proper look at her. Because I now knew the way, Zhang Dong no longer offered to go with me; he visited his toilet, and I visited mine. We were our own people. I enjoyed my freedom, I enjoyed not needing to feel guilty or constrained by his presence. I cherished my only moment of privacy in the day; I even stayed out a little longer than I had to.

For the past few days, Zhang Dong's family had been plotting something together. I sensed from their expressions that it was something important. Zhang Dong didn't seem to want to tell me; whenever I was around, he scowled at his family to shut up. "Why don't you tell your classmate?" his oldest brother's wife blurted out once. Zhang Dong shot her a vicious glare and told her to shut up. I made a point of going through to the next-door room and playing with his nephews.

The closer New Year came, the more conscious I was of how superfluous my presence was. One evening, Zhang Dong's second brother brought home an enormous haunch of pork; the whole family gathered round to admire it. Their New Year's purchases, including the dumplings they'd prepared, were all wrapped in plastic and stored in a lean-to outside the front door, which served as a natural freezer. But every evening at bedtime, they brought the pork haunch inside, to keep it safe from burglars. The rest of the year they never ate so much meat; at most meals it was pickled cabbage and rice noodles sprinkled, at best, with a little chopped bacon. You had to eat their food hot; it became demoralizingly slimy as it cooled. Fresh meat and vegetables such as green peppers were a New Year's treat. Perhaps because it was so cold, I craved meat, great hunks of fatty meat, even though I knew that the family had to scrimp and save for every scrap they consumed. They didn't throw their money around, not because they were mean, but because they just didn't have much. Every time I wanted meat, I felt ashamed of the impulse.

Four days before the New Year, Zhang Dong told me a little mysteriously that he couldn't take me out that day because there was something he had to go and do with his father. That was fine, I naturally said. He was dressed unusually smartly, I noticed; his father had also swapped his habitual slovenly house attire for a navy-blue wool coat ironed into even, faded creases; the buttons were gleaming with gilt, except for a plastic one on the left sleeve that must have replaced one that had fallen off. He'd even shaved, and carefully; the few surviving salt-and-pepper bristles on his chin were pointed out by his grandson. After feeling for them, he tried to pluck them and then went out, coughing as usual. Zhang Dong followed behind, carefully carrying two bottles of wine and a beribboned, boxed gift. I felt particularly oppressed that day, alone in this house that wasn't mine, waiting to be fed; but neither could I complain at being neglected. At midday, Zhang Dong's older sister-in-law told me in a whisper that Zhang Dong had gone to meet his fiancée. "It's all been agreed for ages now, but we've been waiting for him to come home so the two of them can meet." "Whose fiancée?" I asked stupidly. "Zhang Dong's, I told you. His father's getting on and he wants to get it all sorted so he doesn't have to worry. Don't be angry that he's gone out without you." "Of course not," I quickly said. She looked anxiously at me: "Please don't let on to Zhang Dong that I told you, or he'll shout at me. I think he's worried about his classmates laughing at him." "Does Zhang Dong shout too?" I asked her, surprised. "After his father, he's got the worst temper of all of them," she replied.

The two of them didn't return until dusk was about to become night. His father, who had clearly had a lot to drink, was shouting even more than usual, yelling at his wife to get the bed ready because he wanted to go to sleep. "What about dinner?" she asked. "My fair lady," he suddenly sang out in operatic style, "I am replete." Zhang Dong also seemed to have been drinking; he was flushed red down to the base of his neck. He sat on the edge of the bed, staring straight out in front of him. The family gathered in the central room to discuss the day. A general air of satisfaction prevailed; everyone seemed perfectly content with how the introduction had gone. (And indeed, Zhang Dong married her as soon as he graduated; the following year, they had a daughter. Zhang Dong's father was delighted: he had wanted a granddaughter as well as the two grandsons he already had, and his youngest son had duly obliged. The year after that, Zhang Dong's father died happily of myocardial infarction.) To enable them to speak freely, I put on the family's overcoat and headed out. Though I'd originally intended to visit the toilet, I found myself wandering farther and farther away.

Asking for directions at every block I passed and after several changes of bus, I finally found my way to the train station. All the tickets going south for New Year were already sold out, but by paying an extra fifty *yuan,* I secured a ticket to Shanghai for the day after tomorrow from a scalper. Although there was no seat with it, I felt much happier once I had the piece of paper in my hand. By the time I got back to Zhang Dong's, it was nine o'clock (I lost my way in the darkness and snow; it was only the children's hospital that gave me back my bearings). Zhang Dong's mother, sisters-in-law, and nephews were sitting under the lamps; the table was still laid for dinner. The moment I stepped in the door, they all relaxed. Where had I gone, Zhang Dong's mother scolded me, and why hadn't I told them? All the men had gone out looking for me, even Zhang Dong's father. Appalled by the trouble I'd caused, I decided not to tell the truth—I said I'd just gone out for a stroll. The older sister-in-law told me that I needed to be more careful: Harbin wasn't safe; there were a lot of muggings, especially of people who weren't locals. I could have been stabbed to death, buried under the snow, and no one would have been the wiser until spring. While they were telling me this, Zhang Dong's father came back, took off his hat, and brushed off the snow. After staring silently at me, he went into his room. His daughters-in-law quickly stood and moved their stools to let him by. I also got up as fast as I could, pressing myself against the wall. After another while, Zhang Dong and his brothers came back separately, their noses bluish white and red with cold. The younger sister-in-law went to the stove to warm up the dinner because no one had eaten yet. Zhang Dong's mother told the two children to go straight to bed. They didn't want to go: my absence had meant they could stay up later than usual. While we ate, Zhang Dong's father coughed rhythmically next door. Zhang Dong's mother remarked, a little peevishly, that he must have caught cold. I felt horribly guilty. I wanted them to yell at me, to ease my conscience. But no one would. Zhang Dong and his poker-faced brothers refused to say anything at all. They ate noisily, drank their soup, and blew their noses.

When we finally went to bed, Zhang Dong asked me, in hushed tones in the dark, if I'd gone to the station. "How did you know?" I asked him, in surprise. "Did you get a ticket?" he next asked, without answering my question. "Yes," I told him, "for the day after tomorrow, in the afternoon." Zhang Dong tossed and turned a while without saying anything else. I knew he was unhappy. We were sleeping under a single quilt, and so I felt every ripple of his discontent. But for days now I hadn't been sure whether or not his family wanted me to stay; I wasn't really to blame. While I was being scalded in and out of consciousness by the heated wall I lay against, Zhang Dong rolled himself up into a sitting position and said that I should have told him that I was going to the train station, that he would have gone with me. "Why did you go on your own?" he suddenly shouted. Everyone in the house would have heard him. I also quickly sat up. After some groping beneath the quilt, I finally found his arm and tugged at it placatingly. I hadn't planned to go to the station, I told him, it had just happened. He remained disconcertingly silent, awaiting the next stage of my explanation. It's true what they say: that one lie leads to another and I now had to explain a whole spectrum of falsified coincidences to Zhang Dong. Foggy with sleep, I decided to follow the narrative drift of the half-waking dream I had just been having. "Do you remember the *ermao* we saw the other day? I'd gone to the children's hospital and was about to head home when I saw her rushing past me to the streetcar stop, where the number 41 was pulling in. She seemed to be enveloped in perfume; I reeled from the smell. She stood first by the back door of the streetcar, then ran up to the front and got on. If I didn't get a proper look at her this time, I thought, I'd never get another chance. I squeezed on just as the doors were about to shut. I tried to edge my way to the front, but it was very crowded, and everyone was swollen with clothing. Though I craned my neck forward, she was hemmed in on all sides. All I could see was a row of hands clinging onto the supports from the ceiling. But I was sure I recognized her hand, its translucent skin threaded with pale blue veins. I had the strange idea that it wasn't blood inside them, that it was some kind of half-Russian moonshine. Some people got off at the next stop, and I grabbed the opportunity to move up in the vehicle. I felt I was getting closer and closer, that soon I could feast my eyes on her. When finally we were shoulder to shoulder, I wondered whether I should pluck up the courage to speak to her. As I dismissed the idea, she got off; I went on following her, keeping a careful distance all the while so she wouldn't notice. When she walked, I walked too; when she took buses, I took the same ones. When it got dark, I narrowed the distance between us to avoid losing her; when the streetlights came on, I retreated a few steps. I never took my eyes off her; it was as if she had branded herself on my pupils. The wind—sharpened with grit and snowflakes—sanded my eyes; but every tear that oozed out carried a reflection of her image. I had no idea where I was and no interest in the points of the compass; all that mattered was that she was in front of me. I didn't realize I'd arrived at the square in front of the station until someone approached and tried to peddle a train ticket." I had exhausted Zhang Dong's patience. "What's so special about a half-breed," he interrupted, lying back down. He tossed and turned a few more times, managing to steal most of the quilt. I didn't know whether or not he believed me; I'd managed to convince myself.

Two days later, still objecting strenuously to my early departure, Zhang Dong's family presented me with three heads of pickled cabbage as a parting gift. ("You won't get them in the south," Zhang Dong's mother told me.) I got on my train, full of guilty regret and conscious that I faced forty hours of intense, jolting discomfort before I'd be back in Nanjing. After we'd gone back through the Great Wall at Shanhaiguan, the cabbage began to defrost; a trail of vegetable juice snaked persistently across the corridor from where I was standing. The train stewardess was a young woman from Harbin, her voice and features similar to those of Zhang Dong's oldest sister-in-law, which misled me into feeling warmer toward her than she did toward me. In fact, she'd taken a strong dislike to me on account of the decomposing pickles and told me to hang the plastic bag containing the cabbages outside the train window. I was dizzy and nauseous from the train's central heating; I started to feel nostalgic for the far more restrained warmth of Zhang Dong's house. My memories of my Harbin trip coalesced into a single, translucent ice sculpture, in the form of my half Russian. The more I thought about it, the more adamant I became that I had seen her statue at the ice festival in Zhaolin Park. Once I'd reimagined her immortalized in ice, my mental image of her became even harder, even whiter—as if she were cut from marble.

Another trickle of water ambled across the aisle. The stewardess now properly lost her temper at me as she aggressively mopped the area. Smarting at the injustice, I looked under my seat but found nothing that could explain the leak. I'd stood for five long hours to get this seat and my calves were still numb from it. Lacking the strength to engage with the stewardess, I closed my eyes and leaned back against the headrest. Five minutes later, she kicked my cramped legs. "Look!" she shouted. I focused my bleary eyes uncomprehendingly on her. I'd seen quite enough of her self-righteous face; I'd already noted that a tiny black mole shone through the thick blanket of foundation on her right cheek—what else did she want from me? She jabbed the mop violently between my legs; when I looked down, I was astounded to find yet another pool of water there. I quickly stood up and began desperately trying to explain to her that it was nothing to do with me—there was nothing under my seat that could have generated the leak. "Well, where is it coming from then?" she asked. "I don't know," I replied. "I've been asleep." The stewardess turned her inquiring gaze on the passengers around me, but as there seemed to be no clear connection between them and the incident in question, they could relax and enjoy their status as innocent bystanders. The stewardess replaced the sodden mop in a lead bucket and then glared suspiciously at me again: "Why is it by *your* feet?" Every passenger in the car seemed to be staring at me. My ears burned; I asked her what she was driving at. The stewardess's forehead knotted with disgust: "You know exactly what." She picked up the bucket and stormed off.

I watched in horror as she disappeared up the other end of the car, contemplating whether to smash open the train window with my head and jump out. A small trolley laden with stewed chicken legs and liquor bottles nudged insistently at my heel; a male steward stood behind it, clutching a handful of filthy ten-cent notes, silently waiting, head tilted to one side, for me to move. I sat down and took some deep breaths. I lifted my right foot and then my left and examined the soles of my shoes; I glanced surreptitiously at my crotch; nothing unusual to report. An old man sitting diagonally opposite smoking an old-fashioned pipe was shaking his head at me when I looked up again, silently warning me not to pick a fight with the stewardess. I almost choked with gratitude at this demonstration of sympathy. He liked to squat on his seat with his shoes still on, like a turtledove, and had been scolded several times for it by the same stewardess, hence his display of solidarity. Feeling marginally better, I leaned back against the headrest once more and closed my eyes. But still I felt anxious; every now and then I'd check under my feet. Even if I managed to sleep, I remembered, I wouldn't be back in Nanjing when I woke up.

Someone was shouting at me. I opened my eyes and discovered it was the old man, squatting on his seat again, his trouser legs rolled up to his knees, revealing the skin—desiccated into fish scales—on his shins. Using his pipe—from which a pouch of tobacco was hanging—he gestured at the area beneath my feet. Another puddle of water had formed and was just beginning to spread.

I had no idea where the water was coming from. I studied the faces of the passengers around me. They all seemed to be delighting in my misfortunes. I dimly sensed that I was trapped inside a conspiracy, a conspiracy that everyone else in the car was in on; it was hopeless. I could either wait for the stewardess to come and scream at me again or I could leave. I chose the latter. By the time I'd stood up, a middle-aged woman in a head scarf had slipped into my vacated seat. There was something almost supernatural about the speed at which she replaced me. When I looked back at her, she immediately rose halfheartedly and asked if I were planning to sit back down. Her flat, open face was so guileless that I couldn't believe she was behind this dastardly plot. I staggered over to the coupling of two cars and leaned against a wall. Since there was no central heating and a significant draught, I had the space pretty much to myself. Even though it was a little chilly, I felt much more comfortable, much less oppressed than I had back in the car. I even fell asleep briefly while standing up. I suddenly thought to go and check on my luggage but heard a strange squelching noise as soon as I took a step in its direction. Looking down, I discovered that I was standing in yet another puddle of water, trickling down onto the receding train tracks through a hole in the metal floor. I stamped my feet, almost ready to cry with agitation. After checking that no one was coming, I squatted down by the pool of clear water. I dipped my finger in and sniffed it. As my finger touched the water, I shivered; it was freezing cold, as if it had just run off a glacier. I thought absentmindedly of my imaginary ice sculpture; had she started to melt on the journey down south? I could think of no other explanation. If I wanted to avoid seeping water all the way down to the Yangtze—and the inevitable social problems this would cause—I would have to forget her as fast as possible. She belonged to Harbin, hundreds of miles to the north; I couldn't take her home with me to Nanjing.

It was New Year's Eve by the time I got back to Nanjing. When the train passed Jinan in Shandong, I started to run a temperature; I could tell I was going to be properly ill. Eventually I managed to stagger to Xiao Liu's, still carrying my three rotting cabbages. I had nowhere else to go; my college dormitory would have been closed. Xiao Liu—around whose mouth a ring of stress blisters had broken out—exclaimed with relief as soon as he saw me. When school ended, I'd written a short letter to my parents, telling them that I wasn't coming home and that I wanted to use the holiday to carry out a "survey of society" (that was the exact phrase I used—it was very fashionable at universities in the mid- to late 1980s). By the time they got the letter, I was already on my way. If I'd asked them in writing first, they would never have let me go. I hadn't told Xiao Liu either because he would certainly have called my mother. The moment they received the letter, my parents got on the phone to Xiao Liu, who immediately rushed to my dormitory but found that the bird had already flown. Convinced that he was to blame for my flight, Xiao Liu apologized repeatedly to my parents, confessing that he had paid me four hundred *yuan*. My migraine-ridden mother was very tough on Xiao Liu for giving me so much money; I was bound to get into trouble with it, she said. As a result of all this, when I resurfaced in everyone's lives, Xiao Liu first shouted at me for a while and then told me to hand over any money I still had on me, for safekeeping. He next went out to call my parents and tell them I was fine and with him. I spent that New Year at Xiao Liu's. For one thing, I wouldn't have gotten to my parents' in time (even if I'd been able to get a ticket) because they were a six- or seven-hour bus ride from Nanjing. For another, Xiao Liu didn't want my parents to know that I was ill. And so a particularly unhappy New Year was had by all in the Liu household. While I lay in a deep, feverish sleep, his wife—holding her nose—threw away my three faithful, decomposed pickled cabbages.

I probably need to insert a little detail here about my relationship with Xiao Liu. He was an old student of my mother's, not a particularly brilliant one but hardworking and devoted. His middle school years coincided with the nadir in my family's fortunes. My father was under investigation (for alleged illicit dealings with foreigners, espionage, possession of a radio transmitter—that kind of thing), and my mother had been banished to a school in deepest rural China to teach physics. No one learned much of anything in the Cultural Revolution and especially not in the countryside; it was hard enough to find anyone interested in either studying or teaching, and harder again for them to encounter each other. Xiao Liu originally came to us not to study but to fulfill an important undercover mission. He had a crashingly bad class background himself because one of his ancestors had been a shopkeeper in the county town and his own skin was too fair (he was the only boy in the school who used vanishing cream, for which he was universally derided). The local party branch had given him a chance to redeem himself by spying on my mother, who was suspected of being my spymaster father's top accomplice. The difficulty in advancing the investigation was that all the other teachers, students, and political activists in the village were terrified of her; she didn't suffer anyone particularly gladly. So Xiao Liu decided to make a living sacrifice of himself and win some political credit by personally investigating her.

Our family was one of the very few at the time to have a transistor radio at home. Xiao Liu promptly dismantled it, hoping to discover the rumored transmitter. Having scattered parts all over the house, he unsurprisingly proved unable to resassemble them, for which my mother ripped several strips off him (at that moment, he was not a radio obsessive; my mother hadn't yet turned him). He next confiscated our dusty piles of old newspapers, went through every back issue of the weekly digest *Reference News,* and was delighted to discover two copies missing (which my father had obviously sold to overseas agents in exchange for foreign currency). His toughest assignment was to try and break our family's code. Both my parents were from south Fujian, on the east coast, and spoke to each other in the local dialect. When my grandmother was still alive, we spoke nothing but Fujianese at home because she didn't understand Mandarin. Fujianese sounds utterly foreign to speakers of other dialects of Chinese; as a result, we were accused of speaking in cipher. The instant my mother spoke a word of Fujianese, Xiao Liu would ask what it meant. When my mother was in an adequately good mood, she would tell him, and he would lovingly transcribe it in pinyin. More likely, though, my grandmother would chase him out of the door with a broom, as she might an impudent chicken; Xiao Liu would then report back to the party leadership about how this Fujianese battle-ax was probably the real ringleader of our den of spies.

Unfortunately, his surveillance work only intensified the contempt in which he was held at school. I will say one thing for him, though: however savage my mother was to him, he just sat there, blushing scarlet, taking it. And as long as no one outside our family was looking, he would fetch water or coal for us.

As time passed, so did our misfortunes. Xiao Liu still often visited, no longer to spy on us, but to learn about radios, on which my mother had got him hooked. He'd gotten into it to begin with for pragmatic reasons: because his family background restricted his study opportunities, he thought he'd learn a skill and open a stall fixing radios. My mother disapproved: a young person should have more ambition, she said. She actually was quite a decent person, ready to forgive the past transgressions of anyone except my father. Xiao Liu, for his part, always felt guilty about what he'd done and repaid her with absolute submissiveness. And as the years went by, we became convinced by the genuineness of his devotion. His own low point came when they started sending students off to work in the fields; whenever he got the chance, he'd run back to our house, utterly filthy, to weep with the frustration of it. My mother would comfort and encourage him; she lent him books to read and even persuaded her head teacher to let him have the waste from the school toilets for his production team. Eventually my mother persuaded this same head teacher to transfer him back to the school as a temporary lab technician; this gave Xiao Liu the crucial time and conditions to make up the study he'd missed and make him believe in the possibility of a life built on knowledge. It was my mother again who made the head teacher find him a place to study in Nanjing. My mother had an extraordinary influence over this unlucky head teacher because he happened also to be my father.

Xiao Liu was a ubiquitous presence throughout my childhood. When I was little, I'd sometimes go into these strange, staring trances and wander blindly off. More often than not, it was Xiao Liu who brought me home again; my mother didn't trust anyone else to look after me. I was less happy about the arrangement: Xiao Liu's only talent, as far as I could see, was his ability to perform handstands, and even those weren't freestanding—he had to prop himself against a tree or a wall. And even then satisfaction was not guaranteed; he often fell over and hurt his neck. He did a handstand to jolly me out of every one of my sulks; he must have done fifteen hundred to two thousand of them through my formative years. After I started school, my mother turned Xiao Liu into an academic role model for me. I later held Xiao Liu responsible for my parents forcing me to apply to university in Nanjing. In the New Year's holiday of my third year at high school (he always came back from Nanjing bearing gifts, to see my parents), he promised my mother that he would look after me if I went to university in the city. As the post-Mao thaw deepened, as their lives got easier in other ways, it was I, and not Maoist mass movements, who became the chief trigger of my mother's migraines; the idea of a common-law guardian keeping an eye on me was a great comfort to her.

According to my understanding, Xiao Liu had precisely zero love life before the age of thirty. After that significant birthday, he finally—after submitting to various pressures and introductions—met short, dark, chubby Lin Zhimin. Unable to decide what to do about her, he took her on a long bus pilgrimage to see my parents, to get their view on the issue. After the lavish meal that my mother had cooked for them, Xiao Liu tiptoed into the kitchen to ask her what she thought of Lin Zhimin. Uncomfortable at the idea of taking responsibility for something so important, my mother muttered something formulaic about how she seemed like a very nice girl. "You don't like her, do you?" Xiao Liu frowned. "Why do you say that?" my mother quickly replied. "I can hear it in your voice," he said. "You don't talk like that if you really like a person." My mother tried to placate him with a change of tone: "She seems like a very nice girl." And so it was, not long after their return to Nanjing, that Xiao Liu and Lin Zhimin registered their marriage. I was in my fifth year at primary school at the time, but I can still remember the wedding banquet clearly. I sat at one corner of a table, listening to the adults' conversation, staring at Lin Zhimin because I had never seen a woman with so much nasal hair and wondering where Xiao Liu had found her. Remembering dimly that Xiao Liu worked in the Soil Research Institute, and Lin Zhimin at the Irrigation Research Bureau, I decided to show off—as a complete non sequitur—by declaiming a term I'd just learned in geography: soil erosion. The adults at the table stared at me. "What?" Xiao Liu asked. Thinking myself quite extraordinarily clever and well informed, I explained the concept. My mother told me to shut up. Xiao Liu much later reminded me of this long-suppressed memory when he was casting around for long-term causes to explain the inevitability of his divorce. I couldn't quite confirm that I'd come out with such a casually damning prophecy, but I couldn't help wishing that I'd pronounced something more auspicious. Perhaps if I'd said "soil deposition" instead, things might have worked out better.

Not long after the divorce, Lin Zhimin remarried: this time, a bald doctor at the workers' hospital. They'd met when Lin Zhimin's right breast had developed a worrying swelling, which the doctor had carefully massaged away. The doctor helped out the family a second time, too. When Xiao Liu's son was in hospital with meningitis, this affable physician kept a close eye on him. Lin Zhimin said he was a distant relative on her mother's side, and Xiao Liu felt blessed indeed to have an in-law in the hospital. Later on, when his younger sister broke her leg, the doctor helped again; and even though Xiao Liu bought him thank-you gifts, he still felt indebted. Unfortunately, this time the ending was less happy: the bone was not reset straight. Even today, when Xiao Liu's sister tries to walk in a straight line, she finds herself going around in circles. This leg—with its outturned knee—permanently soured Xiao Liu's feeling toward that period in his marriage and also toward Lin Zhimin. After they separated, he did not allow Lin Zhimin, or her family, any contact with her son. I didn't hold any personal grudge against Lin Zhimin; while I was at university, I ate many meals cooked by her, and sometimes she even washed my quilt. But because of the way things had ended between her and Xiao Liu, I felt I had to hate her too, in solidarity. A few years ago, I bumped into her at the post office in the center of Nanjing. She instantly blurted out a long stream of consciousness, most of it to do with Liu Gang and about how unreasonable Xiao Liu was being. She asked me to pass on to him that if he didn't let her see her son soon, she'd take him to court. Her face was noticeably more lined, due, I suspected, to her drastic weight loss. She looked transformed: she had a figure, a spark in her eyes. A neutral observer would say that she looked much better. This meeting set me thinking. I had to acknowledge that for Lin Zhimin, marriage to Xiao Liu had been rich in downsides—it had been an occurrence not unlike the swelling on her breast. I concluded that all women with swellings on their breasts should divorce. I also decided I wasn't going to hate her any more.

In all the years we've known each other, Xiao Liu and I have only had one argument, though it was a fairly serious one. It was in 1988, graduation year and time to look for a job. I'd always wanted to go and work somewhere very far away, to get away from my parents and especially my mother. (For years now, I'd had to make certain lifestyle sacrifices to mitigate her migraines.) As my hopes for studying in Beijing had been squashed, I didn't want to lose the fresh opportunity that graduation offered to get some distance between the two of us. And at the time, universities were actually taking into account students' preferences before they assigned them jobs, which increased my chances of controlling my own destiny. On a visit to the Human

Resources Center, I discovered that the farthest away of the few work units taking graduates from my department was a new thermal electrics company on Hainan, the tropical island off China's south coast to which emperors used to exile their worst enemies; I went for it on the spot. As soon as I had handed in my form, I was hired. Now all I had to do was wait for my diploma to come through, and I was off. My mother—186 miles away—knew nothing of the details of what I'd been up to, but she intuited my desire to leave the southeast. It could be no coincidence that soon after, Xiao Liu began regularly popping up in my dormitory to engage me in small talk about my future plans. Though I kept quiet, Xiao Liu made his own inquiries at the faculty office and, through a combination of threats and cajoling, managed to get me transferred back to Nanjing, which would be better for my mother's fragile nerves.

That was a busy autumn for Xiao Liu. Even though he was under severe physical and mental stress, he still made time to unravel the mess I'd got myself into. I cared nothing about that; my resentment at his intervention simmered away until it found an outlet. After graduation, at the height of the fierce Nanjing summer, Xiao Liu brought me boxes and string to pack up my things. I remembered that he was wearing an old white shirt and had a black mourning band around one of his short sleeves (his father had just died of cancer of the gallbladder). His face ran with sweat as he worked, his dust-covered shirt sticking to his body. Because of the stress he had been under, he had put on some weight. I stood there, gazing at his neck shuddering with rolls of fat, brooding on how my dreams had yet again been crushed. I suddenly exploded at him. I can't remember now exactly what I said, but probably what hurt him the most was my calling him a spy and an informer. He straightened up and gazed at me, open-mouthed, the color slowly draining from his face. There he stood, silently shaking his head until his eyes slowly filled with tears. I realized that I'd gone too far, but my roommates were standing around, so I couldn't apologize. Finally, he set down his packing materials, brushed the dust off his hands, and muttered that there was one more box left to tie up. He turned and left.

We didn't see each other for almost two years after that. During this time, I wrote him two, maybe three, letters, hoping that he'd forgive me; he wrote one short reply, telling me he wasn't angry. He'd made a promise to my parents, which he'd fulfilled. Now that I'd graduated, this responsibility was out of his hands, and he no longer had to make me unhappy; I could choose my own way. Finally, he said he was very busy and wished me well in my career. I sensed that he had no desire to see me again. A few times I thought of going to see him, but when I considered how awkward such a meeting would be, I gave up on the idea. Although we both were in Nanjing, I worked in the north of the city, so there was little chance of our bumping into each other.

Our next meeting was at my parents' one New Year. He'd brought his son, and when my mother asked where Lin Zhimin was, he muttered something about her being too busy (by that point, they'd been separated for some time). I noticed that his hair was much grayer than before and that he'd lost weight—it was particularly noticeable when he stood next to his son who, aged eight, was still pale and swollen from the steroids he'd been given when he was ill. You could tell that the boy knew he was not like other children. He had very little to say for himself; his eyes darted nervously about in their sockets; he hardly ate. The visit was very short—Xiao Liu didn't even stay for a meal—and the conversation naturally revolved around Liu Gang's misfortunes. Several times, Xiao Liu prodded Liu Gang's puffy face and then watched as the indentation slowly sprang flat. He wanted to reassure my mother that it was fat rather than just bloat. My mother was mainly worried about whether the illness had caused any cognitive damage. At the mere mention of this, Liu Gang sprinted out of the room and began chasing the family cat, which fled in terror. Afterwards, Xiao Liu and I had a few meetings in Nanjing, all of which were initiated by me; I hoped that we could get back onto our old footing. He tried hard, too, and whenever we were together, an old, easy affection began to return between us, but if ever I tried to speak to him about anything of any significance, this look of defensive reserve came over his face. I realized that some kinds of emotional damage could never be repaired.

So although we got on in a superficially normal way, we didn't tend to meet very often. Later on, I became more peripatetic and for years did not return to Nanjing. So we were less and less likely to encounter each other.

It was at the end of last year that we started to see more of each other, thanks to a confluence of favorable circumstances. A decade had passed since my graduation, and time changes a person. Some things that once seemed very important become less so, while other things are sweetened with nostalgia. And no one made me tenderly nostalgic quite like Xiao Liu, now fifty and still nowhere near even a deputy departmental headship. In those ten years, my own life had changed; my insistence on doing things my own way had finally succeeded in entirely numbing my mother's neuroses. But the greatest change was that I no longer craved travel. After my eleven house moves and Xiao Liu's one, we ended up living only seven minutes' bike ride away from each other. We shopped at the same market; we bought liquid gas at the same depot; we couldn't avoid each other. Xiao Liu had not remarried, and his obsession with computers had given way to an obsession with his son. Liu Gang was now sixteen but was only in the third year of elementary high. He was currently on his second (and not necessarily, his father felt, final) attempt at completing the year. Although very fat still, he was strong and tanned—an appealing physical presence. I was very fond of him, especially when he called me Uncle. Xiao Liu kept him on a short leash, which sometimes made their relationship rather edgy. I felt I'd been here before, with my mother. Because of my instinctive aversion to this parenting style, very often I couldn't stop myself intervening and managed to mitigate some of Xiao Liu's more draconian decisions. Liu Gang and I got on pretty well. When we were alone together, he had a lot to say for himself; it was only when his father was around that he clammed up. Strangely enough, sometimes if I said exactly the same thing that his father said, I would get a very different response. Xiao Liu happily let his son be influenced by me. Although he felt that things had been difficult for his generation, he was basically content with the way things had worked out. Now that he was fifty, he felt that he was set on a certain course in life but that Liu Gang was still young. He could do better than his father (which, presumably, was where I came in). I suspected that Xiao Liu didn't know what sort of a person I really was. When we were together, it was mostly him doing the talking (he spoke of the Soil Research Institute as if it were the center of the civilized world). I said very little about myself, not because I was deliberately concealing anything, but because I feared he might feel that my kind of life was an affront to his.

One evening, something occurred to me while we talked. After a couple of drinks too many at dinner, Xiao Liu sat on the shabby old sofa next to his bed, facing the eleven-inch black-and-white television that he had himself lovingly assembled years before. A group of girls who (allegedly) made their living from fishing suddenly began cavorting about on the screen, to express how ecstatic China's fisherpeople were about the whole post-Mao reform process. The sound was on so low you could hardly hear a thing, because Liu Gang was doing his homework in the sitting room, but I noted with surprise the way in which Xiao Liu's eyes were fixed almost greedily on the scene as if he were ready to pluck one of the girls out of the television. "Have you slept with anyone since you got divorced seven years ago?" I suddenly asked him. Xiao Liu slowly turned to face me (he had hyperplasia, second degree, of the cervical vertebra) and asked me to say it again; he hadn't caught it the first time. He immediately stood up when he'd heard the repeat, stared at me, then shot a question back, smiling defensively: "What made you think of a thing like that?" Glancing uneasily at Liu Gang in the next-door room, he shut the door then returned to the sofa. "Isn't it a normal, practical question to ask?" I said. "Now that you put it like that," Xiao Liu mumbled, looking at his feet, "it does seem like a good question." After another while, he admitted to me that he hadn't. I could hardly believe it: "Not once, in seven years?" In fact, Xiao Liu confirmed, it was ten years, because he and Lin Zhimin had been separated three years before their divorce. I wasn't sure what to say next; in fact, I was regretting having brought up the whole subject and wondered how I could change it. Xiao Liu began smoking one of my cigarettes, squinting at me through the fumes (he'd never smoked in his life). "When you call it ten years, it sounds a long time," he went on, when I failed to say anything else, "but it just didn't seem a big deal. It went by very quickly; I never even thought about it." Now I wanted to change the subject even more badly than before, but Xiao Liu was just getting into his stride.

Going home that evening, I felt I shouldn't have let things get to this point. As my mother often said, Xiao Liu was a good person; it was just that he wasn't very in touch with his own feelings. He was like a spinning top—without a whip, he didn't know where to turn. He had looked out for me so many times; it was time for me to repay the favor. And so I urged him to place the search for a mate at the top of his list of priorities. From now on, I told him, he couldn't spend every day hiding in the Soil Research Institute. He had to get out more. There were a lot more places to look for a girlfriend than there used to be, what with "brides' firms" and singles clubs; and even if he didn't get a result, at least it would be a change of scene. If he was embarrassed, I'd go with him; I had plenty of time on my hands. Intensely moved by my offer, Xiao Liu told me he wasn't worth bothering over at his age; he was quite happy watching women on the street when he went out shopping. I told him he wasn't too old: he had good skin and with a judicious touch of hair dye, he could look twenty years younger. I was telling him the truth, and I told him more than once. Then he used Liu Gang as an excuse: he was worried that his son wouldn't adjust, and in any case he was too busy keeping an eye on his schoolwork. I took the opposite view: one, I could talk to Liu Gang; two, if he had a wife, wouldn't she free up time to help Liu Gang? I had an answer for every excuse that Xiao Liu came up with, until he ran out of them and told me frankly that he just didn't want to go through with it. When I pressed him about it, he got more and more adept at putting me off, and even went on the counteroffensive: Why hadn't I ever married, my parents were always calling him about it, and so on. I told him not to change the subject. But just as you can't turn a determined suicide, you can't marry off a confirmed bachelor. Once Xiao Liu lost his temper with me: I'd never married, he told me, I had no idea what agony it was to live with the wrong woman. "Find the right woman," I riposted. "Easily said," Xiao Liu rejoined, "harder done. Anyway, who'd have me?" I asked him what kind of woman he actually wanted. "Don't laugh at me," he eventually blurted out, "but someone just like your mother." I was genuinely lost for words; I'd always thought that my father was the only man in the world who could put up with her. "When we were at school," Xiao Liu went on, "everyone in my class was in love with her. We all thought she was our ideal woman."

*

A few final words about the inspiration for this story. Early one morning last December, I had a dream. The afternoon before, on the fifth of the month, I'd arranged to meet a friend at the Jiangsu Exhibition Center in Nanjing, after which we planned to go to the People's Hospital to visit an older friend of ours, who was in for a cataract operation. I didn't mind when my friend kept me waiting as usual; I sat down on the barrier between the road and the pavement, studying the sky, the traffic, the girls going past. It's been a lifelong hobby of mine. But as I did so, I felt someone else was watching me from behind. To begin with, I didn't care; it seemed fair enough that an inveterate watcher should also be watched. But eventually I turned around and discovered that it was a young albino girl standing by a newspaper stall. Her hair and eyebrows were the palest blonde, her skin a pinkish gypsum-white and scattered intermittently with light-brown freckles. Her eyes—squinting in the sun—shone with a naked desire. When our eyes met, she immediately turned away and pretended to rearrange the magazines on the stall. On realizing that I was still studying her, she fled into the crowd. I overheard an exchange between two people who saw her push by them. "Was that a foreigner?" one was asking. "No, an albino," the other one snapped impatiently back. That evening, reading in bed, the whole scene came back to me, and I was sure that the memory generated the dream I had the following morning: I was following an old, crumbling wall along a lake at dusk while a flock of birds rested on a tree growing out of a crack in the wall. I looked around me, wondering why the place was so deserted, when suddenly I spotted a girl staring at me. I recognized her as the half Russian I'd seen all those years ago in Harbin. She hadn't changed at all, except for her sapphire eyes, which seemed to burn with a grievance I didn't remember from before—as if she were reproaching me for not having looked at her for so long, for not having thought of her. I realized that she was right: I hadn't thought of her for a decade—not even once. I should have.

I should thank Xiao Liu for how clearly I recalled this dream, because his phone call woke me from it. He knew my rhythms and wouldn't usually ring me early in the morning unless there was an emergency. He wanted me to talk to Liu Gang as soon as I could. He had been rather secretive recently, and Xiao Liu was worried that he was in contact with his mother. So he'd tailed him for the past twenty-four hours and had discovered instead that his son had been on a date with an equally overweight female classmate. Xiao Liu was almost insane with rage: he swore that if Liu Gang managed to finish school now, he'd eat his own head. Though I had no idea how I would go about it, I accepted my mission—what choice did I have?

DA MA'S WAY OF TALKING
THE MATCHMAKER
THE APPRENTICE
THE FOOTBALL FAN
XIAO LIU

MR. HU, ARE YOU COMING OUT TO PLAY BASKETBALL THIS AFTERNOON?

REEDUCATION
THE WHARF

I have only one motive in compiling the following narrative: to clarify everything that has happened. In so doing, I have no intention of justifying what I have done. I know that everything I have achieved in my career goes for nothing now, that my reputation is destroyed. But I'm past caring. All I want to do is to explain how it came to end like this. I'm not going to ask for your sympathy because it wouldn't mean anything to me. I'll be sixty-five this year: even if this hadn't happened, my life would still be almost over. And because I haven't long left, I no longer care about how I am remembered, about things like honor, glory, or disgrace.

Time flies, as the cliché has it. Before I retired, I didn't really understand this: every day I was busy with this or that—I didn't have time to think hard about anything. That all changed after I stopped working. I felt like a horse finally out of harness, suddenly able to wander wherever it liked. I didn't need to listen to anyone's orders—not even yours. Take it from me: the one thing that elderly people fear most is having too much time to think, because the minute you start to think, you start aging at a terrifying speed. I think that over the past five years I've gone downhill much faster than over the past fifty years put together.

How should I sum up my life experience? I've led a fairly quiet, sedate life compared with many people my age. I won't say I've been particularly fortunate, but neither have I been particularly unfortunate; I've seen many unluckier than I. Take the question of politics for one: all those campaigns, all those sudden changes of direction of the past fifty years—no one ever denounced me, and I never denounced anyone else. For this alone, I should thank the fates for having been kind to me. I'm not a complainer, you see: if you don't believe me, you can go and ask around at my old school. Before I retired, the other teachers banded together to protest to the headmaster about their medical insurance—but I didn't join them. It wasn't because I thought I was above all that or that I don't care about money. It's just my nature. I don't like to complain, whether it's about my superiors or about life in general.

But as I've reviewed my past over the last couple of years, I've started to feel like I was suffocating. I suddenly felt that for decades, I haven't been living the life I should have led—that I've betrayed, that I've wandered too free and far from my true destiny. I've realized this far too late, but that's why I'm now determined to explain everything, from start to finish. I know it won't achieve anything, of course, but I can no longer remain silent.

I'd better begin at the beginning. As you already know, my full name is Hu Gaoyi, and I was born in Wuhu, in southeast Anhui, in 1934. After I graduated from Nanjing Normal University in 1958, I was assigned to a job in Yicheng County, in Shanxi Province. Back then, it had only relatively recently been promoted to county status—there were just two classes in each year at the elementary high and high school, and about twenty people on the staff (including those who worked in the cafeteria). The size of the campus was only a quarter of what it is today. I taught there for thirty-six years until I retired in 1994: during my time there, I taught math to every class in elementary high and high school—I was a veteran of the Yicheng County education system. I also served one term as municipal councillor, and two as county councillor—I even did a term on the county committee for the People's Consultative Conference. . . . But you don't need to know all this—I'll pick out the important parts of the story and try to be as brief and to the point as I can.

I was twenty-four when I began work; back then, people thought you were no longer young at that age, and I was soon introduced to my future wife, Qiu Shujuan, through mutual friends. She was two years younger than I was, born-and-bred Yicheng, and taught Chinese language and literature at Primary School 57—what's now called the City Primary School. We married not long after we'd met. My wife's health was poor even then, but although she was often suffering from one ailment or another, there was an air of great refinement about her. My colleagues joked that I'd found myself a proper Lin Daiyu.* At the time, I was delighted with the match, but after the marriage, I started to realize its drawbacks. My wife was a chronic invalid: the number of days in each year when she actually felt perfectly fit could have been counted on the fingers of one hand. And so the management of our household fell entirely on my shoulders. But I cared little about that. Far more worrying was the fact that my wife seemed unable to have children. We tried hard for three or four years: we saw all kinds of doctors and tried all kinds of medication, but she never managed to keep a baby. Every pregnancy ended in miscarriage, and her health got even worse as a result. I felt we couldn't go on like this: I couldn't be so selfish. So we gave up on the idea.

My wife felt desperately apologetic about this, but I never complained to her. If I were to start complaining—well, I had a lot of other things to complain about first. Two years after we married, I suddenly noticed that my parents-in-law bore an uncanny resemblance to each

* The sickly, poetry-loving heroine of one of imperial China's most famous novels, Cao Xueqin's *The Dream of the Red Chamber*.

other: they had the same long nose, the same long face. They were like a pair of twin horses. After further investigation, I eventually discovered that the two of them were first cousins. So there was a reason for the weakness of my wife's health: it was congenital, the fault of inbreeding. At the time, I felt like I'd been deceived: the whole family had played me like the outsider I was. But we were married now: the rice had been cooked, as the expression goes. Even if it were only half cooked, it was still a pot of rice. And my wife was such a fine, gentle person—what good would it have done to complain? I accepted my lot.

Confucius said that there are three ways of being unfilial, of which failing to produce descendants is the most serious. You can perhaps imagine the kind of pressure that the two of us felt under as a childless couple back in the China of the early 1960s. I took a more relaxed view, but my wife was fixated on the idea. She was a very maternal person—as soon as she saw other people's children, she'd slip them sweets. And so she and I decided, after some discussion, to get someone to help us adopt a child. And that's how we came to have our son, Hu Qiang—Strong Hu—in 1962.

Qiang was an illegitimate child; his natural mother was called Fan Hong, and she'd been eighteen or nineteen when she'd had him. Apparently, she came from one of the villages around here and had graduated from the Yicheng County school. We never discovered who the father was, nor did we try to find out.

The adoption was managed by a relative of my in-laws who worked at the hospital. My heart skipped a beat when I was told that the boy's mother was Fan Hong; my wife was also very hesitant about agreeing to accept him. The whole manner of his birth was fantastical almost beyond belief. Qiang came into this world after his mother tried to drown herself. Back then, for an unmarried eighteen-year-old to find herself pregnant was an unimaginably scandalous thing—especially in a backwater like Yicheng. It's probably hard for you to understand, but back then, suicide was truly her only option. So on November 5, 1962, the day on which my son, Qiang, was born, his natural mother, Fan Hong, jumped into the town's freezing canal. Two passing farmers dragged her out and took her to the hospital; although the mother died, the child miraculously survived. There's one other, extraordinary detail I'd like to add here—though it will sound more like fiction than fact. Even though the farmers, after great physical effort, managed to drag Fan Hong out of the canal, they couldn't carry her on to the hospital. This was 1962, don't forget: because of the three years of natural disasters following the Great Leap Forward, the whole country was still stricken by famine, and everyone was dizzy with hunger. So it was hardly surprising that the two farmers alone lacked the strength to carry her anywhere. They had no choice but to lay her down on one side of the road and sit down to wait until eventually two more farmers came by. The four of them together managed between them to pick up Fan Hong. If it had not been for this delay, she still might have been saved. But then again, looking at things from a different angle, if she'd been revived, we wouldn't have adopted the baby. My wife regarded the birth mother's ignominy as inauspicious, as taboo. Once the mother was dead, however, the disgrace followed her to the grave, and the child was free of her bad luck.

Although Qiang was born prematurely, he was a strong, sturdy baby, with a large, squarish head. Because of her parents' blood relationship, my wife—I heard—weighed only three pounds five ounces at birth, so she was instantly entranced by Qiang, who weighed in at more than six pounds. All the same, I was the one who did most of the work for the baby. But it should be said that Qiang brought us a lot of happiness in those early years. After he came into our lives, I didn't know a moment's peace or rest; my life seemed to be stretched tauter and tauter by all the tasks I had to complete. I now had to look after our son as well as my wife; sometimes my parents-in-law needed help, too—and I had to do my job, of course. Every day I was spinning around like a top. But then, I've often felt that humans have a lot in common with spinning tops—the faster you spin a top, the better it turns. I was young then and in good health; being busy was good for me.

There's one extra detail I might as well slip in here—and it has something to do with Fan Hong. The year after my wife and I were married, for a while I felt very oppressed by my circumstances. Not only could my wife not have children, she couldn't cope with normal marital relations, either. I just had to put up with the situation. It was a time of famine: no one had enough to eat, so logically speaking I shouldn't have had the strength to think about anything else. The strange thing was, though, that the hungrier I was, the more I wanted the other thing. I don't know what it was like for other people, but now that I think back to that period in my life, the two kinds of hunger are inextricably linked in my mind. You'll think me strange, but even now whenever I read the phrase "the three years of natural disasters" in books or newspapers, a strange excitement comes over me before I think about the more conventional political associations of the period—Mao Zedong or Soviet revisionism. My wife would never refuse me, but every time we were done, I hated myself, seeing her lying there half dead with exhaustion. What made me even more uncomfortable was that my parents-in-law could detect the after-effects in my wife's state of health and would take to warning me in a painfully roundabout way that I shouldn't be too regular in my demands, that I should consider Shujuan's well-being. Whenever they broached the subject with me, I felt wretchedly exposed—like I had no place to hide.

Eventually, I came up with a solution: every afternoon, after work, I would go to the sports field to play basketball with my students, to exhaust myself by pounding around the court before going home to make dinner. I was pretty good at basketball; I jumped well and was a decent shot. In fact, I was much better than the school sports teacher. As long as I was playing, there'd be a big audience of students. And that was how I got to know Fan Hong. I never taught her: she only had one more year to go at high school, and I was teaching at the elementary high at the time. She was something of a tomboy. She spent most of the time on the sidelines watching, but from time to time, if there weren't enough players, she'd step in to make up the numbers. I seem to recall she was on the school track-and-field team: she was well built, big boned, with pink cheeks; she was a picture of youthful good health. When she played basketball, her breasts would bounce distractingly, and by the time you'd let yourself think about them, she'd have dribbled past you. My behavior toward her was beyond reproach: this was the 1960s, remember, and in any case I wouldn't have done anything to hurt my wife. But I must admit that Fan Hong fascinated me; she was a completely different kind of woman from Shujuan. I'll remind you again that this was the 1960s: you have to have lived through it to know how tough it was. During the famine, many women stopped having their periods because of malnutrition, and they'd get a certificate from the hospital, authorizing them to buy rice chaff cakes. Rice chaff cakes were pretty empty nutrition; they weren't going to give a woman much of a healthy glow. So a girl like Fan Hong was a rare sight: to look at her made you feel first warm—and also somehow weak. But really, I hardly knew her, and she always addressed me as Mr. Hu. If I bumped into her at school, she'd ask me if I was going to play basketball that day. "Of course," I'd reply. And that was the long and short of our relationship.

We only met once after she left school, on a street in town. If I recall correctly, that was also the only time we met outside school. As I was walking home with some shopping, I heard someone call out to me from behind. When I turned around, I discovered it was Fan Hong. She hadn't changed, I thought, except for her hair—she'd taken to coiling her braids around her head. Back then, she was a temporary worker in some factory in the city and was already getting a reputation for herself—rumors had even reached the school. So when I saw her, I felt rather anxious: I was worried about people gossiping if they saw us together. After exchanging a few perfunctory sentences, I made an excuse and rushed off. I noticed that there was something a little unusual, a little strange in the look that she gave me at the end, which only added to my sense of panic. I ran off without even shaking hands.

My wife utterly doted on Qiang, and we spent all our savings on ensuring that he got enough to eat. Children these days think of something like powdered rice as pretty poor stuff, but it was a luxury back then. I thought up a way to get someone to buy packs of ten boxes for us from Nanjing from time to time. You needed coupons to buy anything, and they were unbelievably hard to come by. When my wife lay on the bed, cradling Qiang in her arms, her face glowed with the pride and joy of a woman who has just given birth. And I made it my business to look after her as I would a postpartum mother. Whenever there was enough money, I would buy chicken and fish to make her soup. She liked to have Qiang suck on her almost concave breasts. I felt conflicting emotions about the situation: on the one hand, of course, I loved the boy, but on the other hand, I couldn't forget that he wasn't my child. The more appealing that Qiang became, the more I craved a child of my own. This is a normal enough feeling: I'm sure you can understand it. But then something unexpected started to happen: as Qiang suckled at her, my wife's breasts did indeed start to swell, and her health in general picked up dramatically. In six months, my wife's physical strength grew steadily; she got some color in her cheeks. And so we decided to try once more to have a child of our own. My wife entered into the process full of confidence and optimism, and in the spring of 1964, she gave birth to our daughter, Hu Lan. Even though Shujuan was utterly exhausted by the trauma of the birth, we both were overjoyed. I now had a son and a daughter. I felt I was the luckiest man in the world, and I didn't even notice all the extra work it brought me.

After having Lan, my wife was always reminding me that we had to be completely fair in the way we treated both children. She didn't need to tell me: we were educated people—there was no way we were going to shortchange Qiang. Although she didn't have much milk, my wife always kept half of it for Qiang. The left side was for Lan, the right for Qiang, even though at the time our son was already two, with almost a full set of teeth. My wife insisted on doing this, though, because she was afraid that otherwise Qiang would not feel close to her. With this most basic expression of the principle of fair shares, everything else fell into place: everything that Lan got, Qiang got too. My wife and I spent all our salaries on our children; each month, we had just enough to get by, though not a cent was left over. But as my wife said, "What does money matter, as long as the children have food to eat and clothes to wear?" This became the motto of our household. I don't remember buying myself anything while the children were growing up: I wore the same old Mao suit for more than a decade and ate nothing but the children's leftovers. Shujuan had no choice but to medicate her ill health far less than before. If it were an everyday kind of an ailment, she just put up with it without seeing the doctor. If possible, she went without medicine—all in the interest of saving a bit of money to pay for the children's food. My father-in-law had a pension, and sometimes he gave us a bit of money, but it was negligible and mainly went on food and clothes for the children.

We worried a lot about how withdrawn Qiang was. He'd grown into a silent, sullen boy. If you gave him something to eat, he'd eat it whether or not he was hungry. In fact, he'd just keep eating—he never knew when to stop. He'd eat himself to death, given the chance. So my wife always kept a careful eye on him: when she thought he'd eaten enough, she'd shout "full," and he'd know to put his bowl down. It was a kind of illness: in Yicheng, they called someone like him a "hungry ghost." You don't tend to see it anymore, but back then there were a lot of people like that. There was no medicine to cure this illness—it was endemic to the famine-stricken era we lived through—and there was no point in trying to treat it, anyway. People slowly grew out of it. Because of this eating problem, we didn't feel comfortable letting Qiang go to nursery school, even when other children his age started. In any case, we thought that children didn't learn anything much at nursery school and that it would be best to keep him safe at home with us.

The year that Qiang turned seven, we sent him to start at my wife's primary school, the 57. Although Lan was only five, she was a precocious child, and after careful thought, we decided to send her to school, too. My wife had to use her connections to persuade the school to take her, because she was two years underage. The two siblings were put in the same class. Because my wife and I were teachers, we'd started the children's preschool education very early. We didn't care about the political atmosphere in the country at the time, about the Cultural Revolution; we weren't going to leave anything to chance. We quickly discovered that Qiang was hopeless academically; you could tell him a character ten times, and he still wouldn't remember it. Lan, who was two years younger, would remember it instantly. The differences between them became even more marked after they started school: Lan was a quick, bright student, always at the top of her class, while Qiang's marks always languished near the bottom. Sometimes I couldn't help think that Qiang's natural father must have been a complete idiot. My wife told me not to worry: "It doesn't matter," she said. "Sometimes it's simpler to be stupid."

One day when they came back from school—it must have been in their third year at primary school—I remember noticing there was something not quite right about the look on Qiang's face. I immediately guessed that someone had said something to him. But you could never get Qiang to talk. However many times you asked him what he was thinking, what had happened, he would say nothing.

One day that summer, 1971 it was, with the holiday just around the corner, my wife had gone back to my parents-in-law's house to help them with something or other. I'd made dinner and was waiting for the children to come back from school. Hour after hour, they failed to appear. At about seven o'clock that evening, Qiang returned alone, covered in dust and grime. I asked him where his sister was; he told me he didn't know.

We later learned that our daughter, Lan, only eight years old at the time, had fallen into the canal and drowned. We were devastated by the tragedy; my wife completely collapsed, and I was close to a nervous breakdown myself. I was convinced back then that Qiang had deliberately taken Lan to the canal to play, but as usual he wasn't saying anything. I fell into a rage and began thrashing him with a stick. It was the first time I'd ever raised a hand against him, but I admit I probably beat him pretty badly. My wife struggled out of bed to restrain me. "We've already lost Lan," she said. "If you beat Qiang to death, what will we have left?" All kinds of rumors about Lan's death circulated around town; everyone had an explanation for it. Some even said that it was retribution for our having neglected and mistreated Qiang—that we'd got what we deserved. An old neighbor told us that Qiang was an ill-fated child and that we should send him away before he brought us more bad luck. Cowed by my beating, Qiang ran to hide whenever he saw me; he would tremble if he even heard my voice. My wife protected him, and we often had arguments on account of it. After particularly violent fights, she would take Qiang back to her parents' house. But all this went on for only a short time; soon I recovered my equilibrium. After all, he was just a child, and children are innocent creatures.

After Lan left us, the spark went out of the family. My wife's health never recovered; from this time on, she rarely made it to work—two years in every three she would spend invalided at home. Qiang became a great worry to her. Although he seemed like a guileless, uncomplicated child, in reality he was a liability. He barely got through primary school and then middle school. As teachers ourselves, we felt thoroughly ashamed of his weak academic performance. It was only by mobilizing the connections we'd accumulated over the years as teachers that we got Qiang through high school. In 1980, he took the high school exam and got 200;* the next year he tried again and did even worse. My wife wanted him to repeat his final year and retake the exam, but I told her to forget it; we shouldn't make the child suffer any more. We then decided to let Qiang look for a job, but he didn't manage to pass the exams for the vocational path either. What were we to do? What could we do? Our only choice was to start bribing people who could help us. To help Qiang with his studies and with finding a job, my wife and I went cap in hand to one well-connected person after another until we'd lost count of the number of times we'd had to abase ourselves for our son. Suffice it to say that we were pretty thick-skinned by the end of it. Finally, Qiang managed to get a job as a builder at an architects' practice. But before the year was out, my wife couldn't stand it any longer: she felt the work was too hard and discussed with me the possibility of helping Qiang get another job. Back then, cooks were in demand again: there were suddenly restaurants in need of them. We thought it was a decent profession to get into. For one thing, Qiang had some aptitude for it; for another, if he could get through a course, he would have a professional qualification, a vocation. And so we tightened our belts again and paid for Qiang to go to a culinary school on the east coast. For once he didn't disappoint us; he graduated after six months. His return back west coincided with the opening of a big new restaurant at Yicheng. It needed staff and Qiang was hired. This time, we didn't have to go to any trouble on his behalf; he got in on his own merits.

* The maximum would have been around 750; decent scores began in the 500 to 600s.

I remember we spent that New Year's Eve at my parents-in-law's house, as usual. Qiang did the cooking and did it well. As we all sat down to the huge table of food he'd prepared, my wife began to cry hysterically before she'd even picked up her chopsticks. I felt elated and drank a bit more than was good for me. At last, Qiang had a future; there was light at the end of the tunnel for us.

Qiang got on very well at the new restaurant and earned a decent sum every month. He was also very solicitous toward the two of us, relieving many of our financial burdens. We began to enjoy life. But before long, Qiang tentatively mentioned that he wanted to head south, to try his luck in a new part of the country. Not long ago, one of his colleagues at the restaurant had gone to Guangzhou and had written back that there was plenty of money to be made there and plenty of work for cooks. My wife was very opposed to it, but I felt I had to take a broader view. We had to think of the boy's future: if he wanted to go out to see the world, this was to be encouraged. We couldn't expect Qiang to bury himself in a backwater like Yicheng. For sure, it was important to be able to make a living, but it was also a good thing to see more of life. I finally persuaded my wife to let Qiang head to Guangzhou. That was in 1984: the whole country was starting to open up—our son was part of something big and exciting.

Qiang came back from Guangzhou for New Year's in 1985. Though he hadn't made any money to speak of, he did bring with him a woman plastered with makeup. The first thing he told us as he stepped through the door was that he was getting married. My wife and I were shocked speechless.

I could see at a glance that the woman he'd taken up with was a bad lot, but there was obviously no way of splitting them up. Pointing at her stomach, she wasted little time in notifying us that she was four months' pregnant with Qiang's baby. We had no choice but to agree to their getting married, and as fast as possible. If we waited too long, there would be no hiding the bride's expanding stomach. In little more than two weeks, on the fifteenth day of the New Year, we arranged a wedding banquet for them, distributing sweets to the guests to stop their mouths. The legal niceties were completed afterward. My wife fainted twice with the worry of it. Both times she came to, she grumbled copiously at me: if I hadn't talked her in to it, she complained, she would never have let Qiang go to Guangzhou, and we wouldn't have found ourselves in this mess.

But Qiang was far more optimistic than we thought he would be: in fact, he rejoiced that a new life was beginning for him. After they were married, he told us all about our new daughter-in-law. Her name was Li Yanyan and she was a year younger than Qiang—she'd grown up in a mountainous part of Jiangxi Province and had moved to Guangzhou to look for work, where she'd become a chambermaid in a hotel. They'd met at a Cantonese-language class. I wasn't fooled by Qiang's explanations: I knew perfectly well what she was—a call girl of sorts, a prostitute. But what could I say now that she was my daughter-in-law? My wife had led a very sheltered life and was still very innocent about such things; she didn't even know what a prostitute was. In time, she came to think that Li Yanyan was a good thing. After all, it wasn't every girl who'd be willing to settle in a backwater like Yicheng with our Qiang, and she was better than average looking. We had nothing to complain about.

We lived in a two-room, single-story house: one room we used as our bedroom, and the other we'd subdivided into two. One half served as the kitchen; the other was big enough only for a bed. We now gave up our bedroom to give Qiang and Yanyan privacy as newlyweds, while we made do with the smaller room. My wife suffered from chronic bronchitis—very often she couldn't even tolerate the smell of coal. But still we didn't complain that we had to live like this: if life was harder, more cramped, we had to cope—as long as we were still alive, we could put up with anything.

On September 17, 1985, Yanyan gave birth, by caesarean section, to a baby girl who weighed in at more than eight pounds. I named her Xiaolan, in memory of our daughter Lan.

Once Yanyan had unburdened herself of her child, she revealed her true self: she was dirty, vain, lazy, and greedy—there was nothing good to be said about her. Qiang was busy at work all day: he had gone back to working at his old restaurant in Yicheng. I was still teaching. For the past few years, I'd been put in charge of math for the final year at high school, which was a big responsibility. Every day, then, it was just my wife and Yanyan at home, looking after the baby. Though my wife was ready to explode with fury, she kept a lid on her feelings to keep the family together. Yanyan, for example, refused to breast-feed the baby because, she said, it would make her breasts sag. We thought we must be dreaming; we'd never heard anything like this in our lives. My wife protested that she had had two children, and no one had ever warned her about it. "Of course they didn't," Yanyan told her. "What can you expect in a dump like this?" We had no choice but to give the child cow's milk. Yanyan also refused to wash the baby's diapers, saying that it would make her hands rough. I looked at her bony, chilblained hands: they already were the hands of someone with a lifetime of hard manual labor behind her. But there was nothing to be done. We set to washing the diapers ourselves. After six months of this, my wife could stand it no longer, and the house became a battleground. Every resentment, every grievance, came out into the open: every day there was a furious argument in the course of which objects were thrown about the house. I could no longer look my neighbors in the eye when I went out. Yanyan now became vindictive: she raked over everything in Qiang's past, stirring up old memories, old quarrels. But this wasn't what got to my wife most. What was most painful to Shujuan was that in every argument, Qiang always took his wife's side.

My wife died of fury—and of physical and mental exhaustion—in 1988.

I suddenly felt terribly alone. How does the poem go? "Heartbreaking are the waters of the Yangtze; we crossed them together, but we cannot finish our journey together." After thinking long and hard and drawing lessons from the bitter experience of the past three years, I decided to ask Qiang and his family to find somewhere else to live. I couldn't care less if other people laughed at me; I didn't want to be driven to an early grave myself. Qiang stared at his feet and said nothing; a week later, they moved out. I refused to care what happened to them. The only time I saw anything of them was at New Year's or on other holidays when Qiang would sometimes bring his daughter over to see me or take me out for a meal.

After the school found out about what had happened at home, they were very concerned about me. One colleague even busied himself trying to find me a new wife, which I refused as politely as I could. I was getting on—I'd be retiring in a few years. I was perfectly happy as I was. But I'd spent all these years looking after other people: could I adapt to having only myself to look after? Maybe I was someone who needed to be constantly busy, constantly working for other people; maybe it was my destiny. In 1990, Li Yanyan decided that she had had enough of Yicheng and ran off without a word, abandoning her husband and daughter. A dejected Qiang brought Xiaolan over to my house. "It's the best thing that could have happened," I told him. "She was a bad woman—you're well rid of her." But Qiang wouldn't listen; he insisted on going after her. I became furious: "Where are you going to go looking?" I shouted. "She could be anywhere." Qiang did not argue with me, the tears trickling down his face. It pained me to see him like this; I'd no idea that this dim-witted son of mine could be so sentimental. I knew that Qiang had already made up his mind. He didn't have many ideas, but when he did get one, he held fast onto it; nothing or no one could deflect him. In other words, I had to agree to look after Xiaolan for him. He packed his bag that very day and set off; I never heard from him again. I don't know whether he found Li Yanyan or even if he's still alive.

Over the years, I've often looked out Qiang's photograph: the more I studied it, the vaguer he became in my mind until I started to ask myself if I'd ever had a son called Qiang.

It turned out to be an eventful autumn. Like two horses galloping shoulder to shoulder to paradise, my long-faced father-in-law and then mother-in-law passed away within a week of each other as if all were neatly prearranged. They both were a decent age: one was eighty-nine, the other eighty-six. They met perfect, peaceful ends: it made me realize that the two of them had lived very loving, happy lives. Thinking this only intensified my own loneliness.

I became sole guardian of my granddaughter Xiaolan when she was only five. I managed her food, her clothes, her studies. She's now fourteen and about to enter her second year at elementary high after the summer holiday. Only I know the joys and sorrows of the intervening years. When she was little, she was just like my own daughter, who died all those years ago: so clever, such a favorite with everyone. Before she started school, she would come to work with me every day. While I was teaching, she'd play on the sports field. A child without parents is like a seed in the wind: they easily set down roots, grow shoots, flower. After I retired in 1994, I had more time to look after her, and she also became the focus of my retirement. Well, without her to look after, what would have been the point of my existence?

Because they're better nourished than we were, children these days mature earlier. Xiaolan reached puberty around eleven or twelve. The ancients were right in saying that women undergo eighteen transformations. I discovered that the granddaughter I had known so well was turning into a completely different person. But she was also somehow familiar: her eyes, her face, her physique, even her movements—I felt I'd seen them all somewhere before. Then I realized whom she reminded me of: she was practically a carbon copy of her grandmother, Fan Hong. I hadn't thought of Fan Hong for years, but Xiaolan brought my visual memories of her flooding back—it was as if Fan Hong had traveled through time to reemerge into my sexagenarian life. And when I thought of Fan Hong, I thought of basketball, then of the famine, then of the desires that I had suppressed for such a long time. Night after night, I dreamed that I was running around the basketball court; I dreamed of those brief physical encounters during a game. Men are weak, particularly when they are as close to death as I am; I no longer had the strength to resist the bestiality that I had imprisoned inside me for so many years. When Xiaolan was thirteen, I committed the act that will forever blacken my name—the act that negated every unimportant thing that I had accomplished in my life.

That night I was transfixed with fear: my soul was suffocated by consciousness of my crime. All night I knelt before Xiaolan's bed, silently clasping her hand. For some reason the scene of my final meeting with

Fan Hong kept flashing before me. Even though I have forgotten what we actually said to each other on that street almost forty years ago, I still remember that final glance she gave me: that curious, quizzical expression on her face. I didn't give it much thought at the time, but at last I understood it. Fan Hong, I felt, had anticipated this ending decades earlier. With that look, she had gazed deep into my future.

That's all I have to say. I know perfectly well what awaits me. The only person I'm still worried about is Xiaolan: she's only fourteen and has a long path in life ahead of her.

DA MA'S WAY OF TALKI
THE MATCHMAKER
THE APPRENTICE
THE FOOTBALL FA
XIAO LIU
MR. HU, ARE YOU COMI

REEDUCATION

THE WHARF

I was fast asleep at one in the afternoon when I received notification that I was to report back to my alma mater on August 31.

Events of the past decade or more had proved beyond a shadow of a doubt that the moral and political indoctrination that my cohort (the graduating class of 1989) received at university had failed miserably. Taking the view that late was better than never, the government had therefore decided to take administrative measures against us: to summon our entire year back to our respective institutions to undergo reeducation; to begin anew the process of forging us into rustless screws.

The summons was easy enough to issue against those of us who were still in China. In the case of those who had left the country to go abroad, the government exerted pressure on members of their families who were still in the country, hoping this would bring them back to the motherland at the appointed hour. It didn't matter how far away they were: all travel costs would be reimbursed. The parents of those who had passed away were obliged to produce cast-iron proof that their offspring no longer existed. Those unable to attend because of illness had to undergo medical assessment at an officially authorized hospital. The summons clearly stated that we were not allowed to bring with us family members, mobile phones, private vehicles, credit cards, cash, secretaries, luggage that weighed more than 220 pounds, pets, or any equipment of any sort that would facilitate family planning. The document's final and most important clause was that after we had reported back, we would not be allowed to live off campus or to eat out at restaurants; we had to live in student dorms and eat in the student cafeteria. All this was to help our special cohort, now in our thirties and thoroughly corrupted by the ways of the outside world, to concentrate on savoring to the full this opportunity for reeducation. The huge sum required to finance Operation Rebake (as it was officially labeled) was to come from two sources: from a specially authorized emergency fund set up by the Ministry of Finance, and from public subscriptions, including a generous donation of twenty million *yuan* from the Paraplegics' Foundation. For two months, the print and broadcast media had been giving blanket coverage to Operation Rebake; I couldn't have ignored it if I'd tried. I could still remember verbatim the famous appeal made by a representative from the Paraplegics' Foundation at the donation ceremony: "Those with a physical disability are unfortunate. But those with ideological disabilities are doubly so."

At the time, I was optimistic about my chances of slipping through the net. I had cut loose of the state bureaucracy many years ago and had lost all contact with my former classmates. I hoped, therefore, to avoid this personal and political cataclysm by remaining quietly in the shadows.

Years ago, I'd parted with my old state employer on very bad terms. The head of Human Resources in the factory where I'd worked had always had a soft spot for me because he'd had hopes of marrying his daughter off to me. Her difficulty in the marriage market was that she was generally considered too tall and too thin. Unfortunately, back then I had even less idea about what was good for me than I do now, and I refused even to be introduced to her—I just cleared out of the place completely. After I resigned, my personal and political dossier remained in the work unit and I refused to care about it.

Most bystanders warned me I'd come to repent. They were right: later on, I really did regret what I'd done. But not leaving that scurvy workplace, which insisted even on issuing us our personal supply of low-grade toilet paper. No, I regretted missing my chance with the daughter of the head of Human Resources. For before long, our socialist society invented a new professional phenomenon: the fashion model. All those girls who, for thousands of years of Chinese history, had been shunned and marginalized because they were too tall now enjoyed an unprecedented liberation. And so I watched, astonished, as the daughter of my former head of Human Resources transformed herself from Liu Hongmei, a machine operator in a nitrogenous fertilizer factory, to Mimi—a B-list celebrity television model. When Mimi first appeared on our screens, her skinny torso wrapped in a pale yellow towel, her hair glistening with water droplets, grinning so cheesily you could see both her incisors, she looked so upsettingly beautiful I had to close my eyes. But my desire to watch her triumphed over the emotional trauma it provoked, so I opened them again, even though I had to shut them again quite soon after that. This advertisement for a water–heating system ran on our screens for a year, and for that year and the six months following, I barely slept. It was regret—deep, painful regret—that was robbing me of my rest. Yet my prolonged bout of insomnia also brought me fresh maturity and insight. Why was I suffering so much, I wondered? Was it because I had not slept with Mimi when I had had the chance? But when I turned the question back on itself, it became meaningless anyway, because the end result was always the same: I hadn't slept with her. Having thus attained an elevated level of enlightenment, I eventually found inner peace.

But my old head of Human Resources' problems were only just beginning. Soon after her big break, Mimi was hired by a big company that specialized in manufacturing medicinal brassieres. Her nominal job title was company "hostess"; in reality her main task was to give blow jobs to top executives seated in leather chairs around the large table in the presidential boardroom. When it came down to it, this type of work was not so very different from her old job, machine operating in the nitrogenous fertilizer factory: both were forms of semiskilled labor involving serious toxins, requiring supervision (on account of the risk of occupational disease) by the Municipal Federation of Trade Unions. My former head of HR, by then on the point of retirement, had no choice but to watch and weep as his beloved daughter found herself swept along by the murky, corrupt floodwaters of the 1990s. Concealing a vegetable knife in his clothes, he vowed to lie in wait for her executive exploiters at the main entrance to the medicinal bra company, in the course of which vigil someone threw a trash can over his head and subjected him to a brutal beating (mainly kicks and punches) that confined him to a hospital bed for two months.

Not long after he got out of hospital, the head of Human Resources decided to accept a generous retirement package. His final act at work, I understand, was to wipe his bottom on my personal dossier—whether literally or metaphorically, I can't be sure. Still today, I find his antipathy toward me hard to fathom, though someone closer to the facts of the case has offered me two explanations for his actions. First, if back then I had actually married Liu Hongmei, she wouldn't have joined that models' training scheme, and the later series of unfortunate, interlinked events involving her and medicinal bras would not have occurred. So that was one thing for which the head of Human Resources was unable to forgive me. Second, the managing director of the medicinal bras company that gave Mimi a contract looked something like me, especially in the way he walked and smiled. I didn't find either of these reasons particularly convincing, but neither was I planning on personally taking up the matter with my former head of Human Resources. Quite the opposite: when Operation Rebake kicked off, I actually felt grateful to him: without my dossier to hand, they would find it even harder to track me down, and I wouldn't have to return to that armpit of an alma mater of mine.

But the summons was, in the event, personally delivered to me by the wife of my landlord—a woman whose asthma was so bad she could barely leave the house. As she handed it over, she looked me up and down, shaking her head from side to side. There was a grimly pitying expression on her face. I lacked the strength to ask her where this document had come from, how they had found me. I felt dizzy, as if all the blood had left my head. I began to hyperventilate. "Blood, I need blood," I gasped, tapping my cranium with my index finger. Next thing, I fainted.

*

When I woke up, I found myself lying on a very soft, very comfortable bed. My entire body was coated with a fine, sticky layer of sweat; I was slightly, just slightly, hungry and still very muggy in my thought processes. I felt like I could have gone straight back to sleep, had I wanted to. The room I was in was sparsely furnished but neat and tidy; no object looked out of place. The curtains were of a pale, nondescript color; at one corner of the window, the branches of a broad-leaved tree swayed back and forth. A small photo frame made of carved wood sat on top of a chest opposite me. Because the photograph was slightly overexposed, I couldn't quite make out the faces of the people in it. All I could be certain of was that the photograph featured a happy family of three—a couple holding between them a tiny, impish baby. I rubbed my eyes, trying to focus on the image. With his square jaw and gleaming bald head, the man on the left bore a striking resemblance to me. Whoever it was, he was dressed in a black suit and bow tie. The woman on the right wore her lustrous long hair loose over her shoulders; she had a decent, if unshowy, sort of figure and was leaning in slightly toward the middle of the photograph. Because she seemed to be laughing, I couldn't get a clear sense of her features. The coziness of this photograph overwhelmed me like a great tidal wave of saccharine; I shut my eyes to preserve myself from its noxious influence. Just as I was about to go back to sleep, a faint, high-pitched mewling noise broke out somewhere in the room, and the mattress beneath me began to heave gently in synchrony with the sound. Flicking the sleep out of my eyes, I looked cautiously about me. A woman dressed in a woolen top and skirt was sitting at the foot of the bed with her back to me: her face was buried in her hands, her shoulder heaving with emotion. I wasn't expecting this. I shot up into a sitting position. Terror made me less civil than I might otherwise have been.

"Fuck! Witch! What are you crying about? You woke me up!"

A moment later, a piercing child's cry erupted. Twisting around, I discovered a small sleeping bag on the inside edge of the bed from which a stout toddler was struggling, with surprising force, to emerge. I sprang up in fear, and backed defensively up against the wall that the bed was next to. I seemed to have no trousers on, I noticed. At that moment, the woman on the edge of the bed stopped weeping, wiped her tears with her sleeve, and turned around to stroke the child's plump torso with two ringed fingers. "There, there, don't cry, lovely." She was a woman of many textures: she was wearing a red mohair jumper and a black wool pencil skirt; her hair was permed into a bouffant style that looked remarkably like a wig. A few strands had adhered to her tear-stained cheeks, matching the dark, downy hair on her upper lip. The child now lay on its back like an upturned turtle, its arms and legs flailing, crying all the louder. The woman didn't have an ounce of spare flesh on her: it almost scratched your eyeballs to look at her. Her hands were painfully bony, and crisscrossed with bright veins; I feared that even shaking hands with her would inflict serious injury. She bent down to pick up the child, but his weight almost caused her to tumble forward. All this was bad enough in the abstract, but as a matter of urgency, I also had to work out who exactly this woman was. The thing was, I was sure I'd met her somewhere before.

"Who the hell are you? What are you doing here?"

"I could ask you the same thing."

She finally succeeded in picking up the child, but his weight quickly forced her to sit back down on the bed. Eyes still shut, the child began nosing around her chest area like an inquisitive cat and was rewarded (to his great disgust) with a mouthful of mohair. Without using her hands, the woman bent over, removed the mass of red fibers with her mouth and set about chewing it into a small, neat ball. I was spellbound by this feline maneuver. She abruptly turned and exhaled in my direction. Instinct told me to take another step back, but the cold wall behind me cut off any further retreat. I yelped as I felt a sharp, painful twinge in my right calf. She laughed merrily at my discomfort; in fact, she laughed a little too hard and began choking on her amusement, which in turn generated a quick succession of loud, happy hiccups. I was starting to have my own suspicions about who she was, but I still couldn't quite be sure.

"You wouldn't be—Hu Pingping?"

"Just came back to you, then?"

"It's impossible. It can't be true."

But there was no escaping the fact: she really was my former college classmate, Hu Pingping. It was ten years ago, my fourth year at university, I now remembered, that my troubles had begun, when another classmate had bounded up and reported that Hu Pingping was looking for me. Though she was only five feet three inches tall, she weighed 176 pounds, and back in the first year our classmates had nominated her as our cohort's lifestyle representative for this reason alone. Totally oblivious to the irony of her nomination to public life, Hu Pingping diligently served our undergraduate constituency throughout our four years at college. Encouraged by the unanimous acclaim she won for the extracurricular work she did on our behalf, she decided to focus her energies on reforming my own degenerate lifestyle. She almost managed it, too. My appetite for women reached its peak in my fourth year at university: I wanted any and every woman—even the crippled old lady who sold hard-boiled eggs by the entrance to the university. I felt bad after I'd had her, but I still wanted her again. In all, I slept with her four times until eventually she took to avoiding the university. For some reason, though, the only woman I managed to restrain myself from was Hu Pingping. But finally, during an unbelievably boring weekend, I decided I would have her, too. If we made a regular thing of it, maybe I could help her lose weight, as a way of repaying the favor. To my astonishment, she wouldn't let me near her. In the course of a night-long siege that tested the limits of my physical and mental resilience, I succeeded only in stroking her cheek with the back of my hand.

That brief physical contact was my downfall. Hu Pingping thought that it was confirmation of our betrothal and set about publicly laying claim to me. First thing every morning, she would bring breakfast over to my dormitory, pull my curtains open, and force me to get up. If I changed my underpants, she would pass me a bulging envelope the following day during a break between classes, containing the just-discarded underpants, not only washed and dried but also perfumed. Soon, I was almost insane with it; for two weeks, I didn't dare return to my dorm at night.

Eventually, that long winter of persecution passed. One day in spring, another classmate—a girl by the name of Li Xia, a left-hander, I recall—told me she wanted a word. I knew that she and Hu Pingping were thick as thieves: they slept in the same bunk bed, one on top, one below. In fact, rumor had it that during the winter they shared the same bunk. She hissed at me, in a corner of one of the lecture buildings, that I should take a long hard look at the situation: if I went on upsetting Hu Pingping and the faculty got to hear about it, I could wave good-bye to graduating. I couldn't believe what I was hearing: "What about Hu Pingping upsetting *me*?" Li Xia threw me a contemptuous look: "Don't play dumb. Stop pretending you don't know what I'm talking about. Hu Pingping's pregnant." This is where I started laughing: it was actually funny. I asked (rhetorically) what Hu Pingping being pregnant had to do with me, then made as if to leave. Li Xia stamped hard on my foot to prevent my early exit. "What part of what I just said did you not understand?" she asked, glaring murderously at me all the while. I lost my nerve here, I'll confess; indeed, I was paralyzed with shock. To anyone else, I probably wouldn't have given the time of day, but I had a guilty conscience about Li Xia. Back in our second year, I'd grabbed an unexpected opportunity to sleep with her but had hardly exchanged a word with her either before or after the event. And Hu Pingping, it had to be said, hadn't been looking herself lately. After gaining another twenty-two pounds, she was almost wider than she was tall. She looked terrible and had completely withdrawn into herself as if consumed by thoughts of her own troubles. Rumors swirled about her growing abdomen; with every day that passed, the gossip seemed to become more lurid. It was necessary, I felt, to point out some of the facts of the matter to her, which I chose to do one evening in one of the classrooms given over to private study.

"So. You're pregnant, I hear?"

Hu Pingping suddenly began to weep softly. The room was full of other people; they began sneaking glances over at us.

"What the hell are you crying about? Look: it's got nothing to do with me."

Oblivious to my words of reason, Hu Pingping now flung herself over the desk and began weeping more loudly. Because she was crying so hard, she choked a little and began hiccupping in between her sobs. I stuffed the books piled on the desk in front of me into my bag and stood up. Sensing my intention to leave, Hu Pingping looked up, her face awash with tears. "For once in your life, face the consequences of what you've done!" she screamed. I felt dizzy, as if all the blood had left my head. I began to hyperventilate. "Blood, I need blood," I gasped, tapping my cranium with my index finger. Next thing, I fainted.

I tried telling myself to stay calm, but I knew full well that as soon as word of the affair reached the faculty, I'd never be able to talk my way out of it. They'd been looking for an excuse to throw me out for years now; this was a heaven-sent opportunity. And there was no way I could count on Li Xia's discretion: I've never trusted left-handers. In order to calm Hu Pingping down, I took to walking her around the city with a look of ostentatious contentment on my face, as if we were in the full throes of young love. Back then, I remember, the days passed as if they were years; all sense of joy and anticipation about the future evaporated. But then a way out miraculously presented itself. Just at this crisis point in my personal affairs, the demonstrations of spring 1989 kicked off. The protests became more radical by the day until they seemed to engulf the whole country. Our university collapsed into anarchy, and the faculty authorities no longer seemed quite so terrifying to me. Against this conveniently chaotic backdrop, I simply decided to eject Hu Pingping—who now weighed two hundred and twenty pounds at least—from my life. The happiness that this decision brought me, together with the trouble that ensued from stroking Hu Pingping's cheek, are the two events in my university career that, ten years after I graduated, I still remembered as vividly as if they had happened yesterday.

So that was the long and the short of my relationship with Hu Pingping.

The child had stopped crying. "Did I give you a shock just now?" the women in mohair asked, gazing affectionately up at me. Brushing a tangle of thread off my calf, I gingerly sat back down under the quilt. Studying Hu Pingping from behind, I guessed she now weighed no more than ninety-nine pounds—she was slim bordering on the bony, in the style that was currently deemed fashionable. In other words, she was half what she had once been. Given that in the past I had encountered a Hu Pingping who told the truth and a Hu Pingping who told only lies, I hoped that she had sloughed off the deceitful half of her and that she wasn't about to tell me that the baby in her arms had my eyes. I was unable to relax until I had ascertained paternity. (As one of the ancients put it so well, the heart of a woman is like a needle on a seabed—no human can find it.) Putting one foot down on the ground to balance myself, I reached out to pick up the photograph on the chest. After carefully examining the happy family in the picture, I was relieved to discover that the man was not in fact me. "It's my ex-husband. He's emigrated to Australia to start a sheep farm," Hu Pingping explained, her voice devoid of expression. She fell silent, as if waiting for my next question. But I'd run out of things I wanted to ask because—now, as ten years ago—I had no aspirations for our future together. Feeling a touch happier with life, I slipped under the quilt.

"Don't go back to sleep. We've got to go in a minute."

"Go? Fuck, where?"

"We have to go and register at the university for Operation Rebake. Today's the last day for enrollment."

I sat bolt upright again. All sorts of thoughts swirled chaotically around my head. My nervous system had ceased to self-regulate since

I'd received my summons. I'd been yo-yoing between a state of denial and paranoid hallucination; mental equilibrium was going to prove elusive. I closed my eyes and tried to think things through, but nothing made sense.

"I remember now. OK, I have to sign in. But why do I have to go with you?"

"Honestly. We agreed ages ago—don't you remember?"

"Uh, I remember now. But I still have to go home and get my stuff together."

I pulled back the covers, jumped off the bed, and quickly tugged on my trousers. I felt an urgent need to leave this place.

"There's no need. Your suitcase's already here, don't you remember? I've never seen anyone put on trousers so fast. You'd think that's all you've spent the last ten years practicing."

Hu Pingping motioned at the door with her chin. In front of it lay two enormous bags: one on its side, the other sprawled on top. She continued to feed me helpful reminders: "When you brought your luggage over, you told me it was everything you owned. In fact you were worried you'd brought too much: the summons said that our luggage mustn't exceed two hundred twenty pounds. I told you it didn't matter. I wasn't bringing much, so if we put our bags together, we'd be able to get it past them. Then we guessed roughly what they weighed in total, and we thought they might still be a bit over the limit." "Really?" I asked. "Why can't I remember any of that at all?" I was beginning to sound as if I were talking to myself. "Of course, we did. You even made a joke about it." "What was it?" She blushed and said nothing. "Come on," I asked impatiently. "Spit it out. I won't believe you if you don't tell me." Hu Pingping finally reported my own *bon mot* back to me: "You said: Even if our luggage is overweight, I bet *we* wouldn't be overweight."

"What the hell was that supposed to mean?"

"I don't know. You tell me."

I told her I needed to use the toilet and disappeared off to the bathroom to collect myself. I must have spent ten minutes there, considering my options. When I reemerged, I saw that Hu Pingping had placed the child—now fast asleep—back on the bed, and sat down next to him. She then lifted her top and began stuffing handfuls of notes into her bra. "What the hell are you doing?" I asked. "Best to bring some extra money, I thought," Hu Pingping replied without even looking up. "We might need it inside. Well, I won't need it, but I know you've got all sorts of addictions and bad habits. I thought it might help." "Wait a minute," I said. "I don't need you to bring anything for me. Look, I've been thinking. I reckon it's still best if we go separately. You've got a child to look after. You're bound to have hundreds of things to sort out." "It's not a problem," Hu Pingping interrupted. "I've already arranged everything. My parents are going to look after the baby. They'll be here any minute. As soon as they get here, we can go." She glanced at her watch: "They should be here already. They're normally never late." She turned around, undid her belt and the zip on her skirt, and stuffed the final handful of one-hundred-*yuan* notes inside her underpants. She stood up and smoothed down her clothes. "So," she asked me, clearly pleased with herself. "How do I look?" "Your bust's a bit bulgy." Hu Pingping rearranged it slightly: "I don't care. I only care about helping you through this difficult time."

"Look, I appreciate the thought, really I do, but I think we'd better go separately."

Hu Pingping trembled slightly as she stood before me. She glanced first at me, then down, smoothing her jumper and skirt. The room was eerily quiet.

"If that's what you want, then I'm not going to stop you. But would you mind saying 'fuck' a little less often? It's so vulgar."

"Fuck! Why not? The baby can't understand anything anyway, and I'm sure you've heard worse."

"I don't care. I don't want you to keep saying it."

"Why the fuck not? How do you think we got here in the first place? What have I spent most of my life doing?"

Hu Pingping covered her ears with her hands, a pained expression on her face. Watching this, I only got angrier.

"Take your hands away from your ears!"

Soon enough, I calmed down, opened out the luggage trolley propped against the wall, and bent down to lift my backpack onto it. Hu Pingping released her ears, sighed heavily, and began staring reproachfully at me. Her eyes reddened as soon as she began to speak.

"I'll tell you what I feel when I hear you say that word. Remember what happened ten years ago?"

"Remember what?"

"You've a nerve asking me that. It reminds me of that terrible time. I suffered so much. Remember now? Did you ever ask me how I got through it? It almost destroyed me, you know."

"You're not talking again about getting pregnant, are you?"

"What do you think?"

"Ten years, and you're still lying to me. I'm so angry I could kill you."

In fact, I lost my mind. I rushed forward and grabbed hold of her long, chicken-like neck. Her tongue hung out as she gasped for air. I really didn't want to kill her, but I was seriously worried that I might well end up going through with it. I needed someone to stop me. At that moment, blessedly, the doorbell rang. I immediately let go of her, and she staggered around the room, hyperventilating. Ignoring her, I secured my luggage on the trolley and pushed it to the door. When I opened it, I discovered an ill-matched elderly couple waiting outside. Hu Pingping's mother was more than averagely short, with a cleaver-sharp face, small, beanlike eyes, and the muzzle of a lion. This entire ensemble of features—frozen into a look of ferocious, nonnegotiable hatred—was topped by a pitch-black mane of a wig. She was holding an unopened bottle of milk. The father, by contrast, was tall and lean, a handsome, straightforward-looking man; his hair was sprinkled with gray. He was rather pale: from his pained expression, I guessed that he had just endured a savage scolding. The pair of them had clearly been furiously fighting on the way over here, but as soon as they saw me, they pasted false smiles over their faces. Barely acknowledging their existence, I made as if to charge between them. The two of them jumped aside, like frightened birds migrating to the walls of the corridor for protection or, rather, more like spooked geckos. But I was all out of luck. The wheels of the trolley got stuck on the lintel, and the whole thing refused to budge. Having composed herself again, Hu Pingping came over and stood by the doorway as if nothing had happened, her hands folded behind her back. She neither offered to help nor said anything; she just watched me struggling with the mechanism. In fact, all three of them watched. I was bright red with the effort and out of breath. Although raging at the situation, I still couldn't get the thing moving. In the end, I flung down the handle of the trolley in defeat and straightened back up, exasperated with the bloody-mindedness of it all. Sighing with relief, the taller gecko edged away from the wall. Brushing the dust off his hands, he put one of them on my shoulder. "Calm down," he told me. "Take the weight off your feet." I was warmed, persuaded even, by the look in his eyes: male solidarity, perhaps, or the mutual sympathy of the persecuted.

Hu Pingping and her tough-talking mother began circling the room like two hyperactive sparrows that had flown in the window by mistake. "The milk powder's here, the diapers are there, that's the microwave, there's the spittoon . . ." "Yes, yes, I know," Hu Pingping's mother replied. "I'm not your father, you know." Her father and I had settled down on a couple of small sofas in one corner of the room. He silently but hospitably offered me a cigarette and then lit it for me; he didn't take one himself. He gestured at his throat, then made a helpless gesture. I guessed he meant that there was something wrong with his throat and he couldn't smoke. We had understood each other. After another little while, he gestured at the two women chattering in the kitchen and made another helpless gesture. I guessed he meant: beware of women. We had understood each other a second time. I stared steadily at the old gentleman, awaiting his next insight, but he turned away and stared absentmindedly out the window. I'd smoked half my cigarette by the time he turned back to me. He then pointed out of the window and made another helpless gesture. After thinking about it, I guessed he meant: it's a tough world out there. Again, we had understood each other. I began to feel rather oppressed by this social situation. Just then, the old man's gaze fell on the baby sound asleep on the bed. His face slowly lit up. He pointed at the child and then gave a thumbs-up sign. I guessed what he meant was: but things will get better. Children are the future and hope of the motherland. I quickly finished the cigarette. He passed me another and again lit it for me. Again, he didn't take one himself, pointing—as before—at his own throat and sadly shaking his head. We experienced yet another moment of entente: his throat was never going to get better. Just as rain falls and as girls get married, there was no fighting the ways of this world. He gestured again at the two women boomeranging in and out of the kitchen and sadly shook his head. Life was getting worse by the day, and there wasn't a thing any of us could do to change it. When finally the old gentleman turned again to his grandchild, busily dribbling in his sleep, two fat, cloudy tears squeezed out of the rims of his eyes.

Just as we were about to set off, the child woke up and began crying inconsolably. Hu Pingping's mother had to stay behind to look after the baby while her father took us to the station. Just as the elevator door was about to shut, Hu Pingping's mother charged out. "Have you remembered your medicine?" she roared. Then the door shut, and the elevator began to descend. "Did you remember it?" Hu Pingping's father whispered when we reached the tenth floor. Hu Pingping glared at her father, as if reproaching him for bringing up the subject while I was around. I looked away as if I hadn't heard a thing.

When we got out onto the street, Hu Pingping's father insisted on walking ahead, carrying that bag of mine that had defeated the luggage trolley. That left me no choice but to help Hu Pingping with her own suitcase: it had one of those pull cords that meant you could drag it along behind you like a pet dog. I did not want to be seen with her in public and tried to detach myself several times, though without success. It was about two o'clock in the afternoon, and the street was rammed with pedestrians, all jostling one another in their attempts to move forward. While I was getting increasingly irritable, Hu Pingping's father was starting to suffer with my bag—his back was bent like a bow drawn to breaking point. Unable to stand it any longer, I accelerated to catch him up and offered to take over. But he refused to relinquish his burden; on he walked, a few paces in front. I walked up to him again, told him to put the bag down, and proposed hiring a couple of migrant laborers to carry them for us—it would have cost me only a few *yuan*. Although the old man's lips were now blanched with physical effort, he categorically refused. Later on, I understood his strategy. He had resolved to make me walk behind him feeling guilty, intending that I would transfer this feeling of obligation to my interactions with his daughter. I had to admire his paternal instincts even if I didn't appreciate them.

By the time we reached the railway station, his shirt was soaked with sweat. He told us to wait on the platform and watch the luggage while he doddered off to the ticket office. Hu Pingping wiped the sweat off her own forehead with a handkerchief, then fanned her neck with it. I watched, glassy-eyed, as a train moved into the station and the travelers on the platform swarmed up to it, dragging their various bundles of belongings with them. "Do you know what medicine my parents were talking about?" Hu Pingping broke the silence in an effort to lighten the tone. "How should I?" I answered shortly. Hu Pingping's father was staggering his way back out of the crowds surrounding the ticket office. "The pill. Imported from Germany—they're multicolored. The Chinese stuff gives me a rash." "Why are you telling me this? And isn't that breaking the rules?" "It's not a problem. I've put them in a vitamin bottle. We can't make the same mistake that we made ten years ago."

I felt dizzy, as if all the blood had left my head. I began to hyperventilate. "Blood, I need blood," I gasped, tapping my cranium with my index finger. Next thing, I fainted.

*

There was an air of desolation about the main gates of my alma mater, even though they were gaudily decorated with lanterns and streamers—it was as if we were arriving for a celebration that had run its course the previous day. The year's freshmen were arriving at the same time as the old guard registering for Operation Rebake, and the university had accordingly hung two symmetrical, vertical scrolls outside the gates: "Welcome to New Students" (on one side) and "Welcome Old Friends" (on the other). The whole place looked exactly as it had ten years ago: an avenue lined on both sides by plane trees took you away from the gates and into the campus. Their trunks would have taken two arm spans to encircle. Oddly though, the trees seemed if anything to have grown thinner, rather than thicker, over the past decade—a common enough occurrence these days. Each tree had had a slogan pasted on it, though the characters were a little blurred after the recent rain. "Rebaked Sesame Cakes Are the Most Delicious!" read one. I suddenly began to feel hungry.

I was surrounded by animated seventeen- and eighteen-year-olds; they reminded me of a great shoal of fish, just netted onto dry land. I was sure they were pointing at me, whispering about me. The situation made very extremely uncomfortable even while I raged inside that ten years ago, I would have had them all for breakfast. Hu Pingping and I dragged our luggage around behind us, like the lost parents of a new student, unable to discover where our offspring was supposed to register. She seemed very excited. Abandoning her suitcase, she told me to stay where I was and keep an eye on our things while she worked out where we were supposed to be. I sat down on the roadside, watching her head off toward an auditorium. But after only a few steps, an overweight man appeared from somewhere and called out to her in a booming voice. As soon as she saw who it was, Hu Pingping heaved an audible sigh of relief. She rushed over, flung herself into the man's arms, and burst theatrically into tears. I initially assumed he was a relative of hers, but when I took a proper look at him, I discovered he was our political education tutor from ten years ago. Though still balding, he otherwise looked like a new man. Back then, he'd been on constant medication for his diabetes and was never seen without a cigarette hanging from his mouth. To us, he'd seemed more dead than alive. Now, though, he stood tall and straight before me, apparently glowing with health. Hu Pingping turned around to gesture at me and then said something to the tutor. His face grew serious as he glanced repeatedly back at me. She buried her face in his chest and started crying again as if she had a major grievance to get out of her system. The tutor solicitously patted her on the shoulder. I couldn't hear what they were saying, but I could sense that it wasn't particularly complimentary to me. I was beginning to feel as though I was trapped in some sort of conspiracy. Eventually they walked back over to me.

"So you're here at last. Everyone else has already arrived." The tutor extended a hand to yank me up from the ground. His hand was unusually soft; it gave me the strangest sensation—as if I were holding another part of him altogether. But once he had me in his grasp, he seemed unwilling to let go. He stared appraisingly at me for some time, laughing inconsequentially all the while and asking me idiotic questions about my domestic situation. He told me he'd retired several years ago, but when Operation Rebake was announced, the deans had begged him to return on a new contract—to start a new, glorious chapter in his working life. As he related this, his grip tightened. Suffering an almost nervous reaction, I decided to fight back with a more severe grip of my own. Now, handshaking was one of my hidden talents, and with one light clench of my fist, my adversary crumbled. His joints crunched, his plump face twitched, and he relinquished my hand. Changing the subject, though not the expression on his face, he turned to gesture at Hu Pingping as if nothing had happened. "We're lucky we had Pingping here to help out. Otherwise, we wouldn't have been able to track you down, even if we'd looked in all the sewers in China." I gazed questioningly at her, increasingly confused by the direction things were taking. She looked away as if she hadn't heard a thing. Because the embrace between Hu Pingping and the tutor just now had been excessively ardent, her previously pert bosom had been crushed flat. I couldn't decide whether or not to feel sorry for her. "Don't stand there like an idiot," the tutor said. "Let's go and find everyone else. They're all waiting for you." I picked up my luggage, while the tutor pulled Hu Pingping's along so that she didn't have to take anything at all. I was anxious that Hu Pingping, with nothing else to do, would come and help me with my bags, but my fears were groundless. "I really can't wait any longer," she told the tutor, her voice thick with emotion, her hands clasped yearningly under her chin. "Tell me where everyone else is. I'll go over ahead of you two." "That's fine," he replied. "They're in Room 101, Zhongshan Building—do you remember where that is?" "Of course," she said. Hitching her pencil skirt up a little, she cantered off. She ran so freely and happily that hundred-*yuan* notes fluttered out from beneath the hem of her skirt; new students trailed behind her, scooping them up with murmurs of astonishment.

The tutor walked sedately behind with me, telling me frankly that ten years ago, back in 1989, things had looked very bad for him. Both faculty and students had treated him with barely disguised contempt. "On the surface, I got on well enough with my colleagues, but I knew that deep inside they thought I was past it, a fossil." So when his diabetes had gotten worse, he'd decided it was time to give up the game. He didn't have a choice: China was moving on. But then, and against all the odds, a fresh opportunity had come along, and his skills were in demand again. "I'll tell you a funny thing: as soon as I heard about Operation Rebake, all my symptoms disappeared. Even my hair started to come back. My appetite improved and I started sleeping better. Right now, I feel so alive!" This whole speech struck me as so laughable that I had to try and lower its tone. "You should try and seduce one of your students, you know. You might pull it off, this time." To my great surprise, the tutor took my suggestion very seriously. "But who? I'll be honest with you—these students back to be rebaked, they're all a bit past it now."

By this point, we were back at the start of the wide avenue leading away from the main gates to the university. The tutor stopped and pointed meaningfully at the entrance. "What's that supposed to mean?" I asked. "Nothing in particular," he replied. "I just wanted you to take a long, hard look at what you're leaving behind." I smiled, a little uncomfortably: "D'you mean that things are different now? That this is no longer 1989? That this time I won't walk away so easily?" He shook his head vehemently, his jowls trembling.

Neither of us spoke after that. When we got to Zhongshan Building, the tutor told me to leave my bags with the mountainous pile of luggage at the entrance. He said I didn't need to worry about them: in a while, a truck would come and pick everything up. Now abandoning all exercise of free will, I followed him into a spacious lecture hall with tiered seating and fluorescent lighting. As we entered, the tutor shielded me with his own corpulent form while he marched toward the center of the room. "Look who I have here, everyone!" he cried out, stepping nimbly to one side, like a magician revealing a white rabbit. Everyone in the room was dressed in their best and had huddled into groups. They were, for the most part, too busy reminiscing to take much interest in my dramatic reappearance—though a few waved vaguely at me. I wasn't particularly disappointed by my nonimpact. Although I've forgotten many things over the years, I could still remember that I hadn't got on that well with any of them. Indeed, ten years ago, quite a few of them would have enjoyed watching me die in agony.

The tutor brought the register over from the podium and told me to sign in. I've never liked signing registers or forms: for some reason, my hand always shakes so badly I can barely hold the pen. Standing over me, he told me what to put in the different columns until someone shouted for him in the corridor outside, and he went off to find out what the problem was. The final column was entitled "Further Remarks"—I had no idea what to write. Glancing at what my peers had written above me, I discovered that most had gone for the kind of adage more appropriate to epitaphs. "Never forget a good teacher; they shine a light for later generations"; "May my children study hard, and my wife stay virtuous"; "You'll still be my hero twenty years from now." Finding the whole business ridiculous, I left the column blank, set down the pen, and tactfully withdrew up the steps to the final, top row of the classroom's tiered seating. There, I took up my old place—the seat nearest the back door. Everything was just as it had been ten years ago; a decade, it seemed, was nothing. I discovered to my surprise and joy that a calligraphic inscription ("fuck") that I had left on the desktop with a sharp pencil during a "Moral Education for University Students" class was still there; the strokes of my characters were as sharp and clear as they had been ten years ago. But it reminded me how transient humans are, relative to the material world. A cacophony of voices argued around me. With every minute that passed, I became more convinced that I had been lured back into a madhouse:

"Operation Rebake's going to be the equivalent of sending our parents down to the countryside during the Cultural Revolution. People have always said our generation's useless because we've never suffered, we've never been tested by anything. Operation Rebake's going to give us something to say for ourselves."

"The authorities know what they're doing. They've got a plan. They're going to put our marks from each term in a new personal dossier to select a handful of people with leadership potential and give them key national posts to carry the country forward to meet the challenges of the new millennium. It's an opportunity: after all, we're the generation that's going to take China into the future."

"After I got my summons, I stayed up all night watching the stars. The sun, the moon, and the stars all moved together to form Pisces."

I noticed that one other classmate in the room had not joined in the animated discussions ongoing. His suit was crumpled, his hair was a mess, and his face was haggard—as if he were nursing some deep sadness inside him. As I studied him, I struggled to remember his name. In time, he noticed me, too. I nodded at him; he responded only by staring at me. I kept nodding at him, and even flashed him a friendly smile. My overture was counterproductive: he promptly began weeping in great, wolflike howls. Immediately noticing his intense grief, everyone rushed over to comfort him. What was he crying for, they wanted to know. This was a happy day, an opportunity for old friends to get together. He was obsessed with going to America, it turned out. Even at university, he'd been convinced that life outside the United States was not worth living. He had sacrificed everything for his dream, and despite years of struggle, he had not found his way to paradise on earth. But at last, a decade after graduation, he had achieved his life's ambition: he had been granted a U.S. visa. But just as he had set about selling all his belongings to buy a plane ticket, Operation Rebake had begun. Realizing that nothing they could say would do any good, everyone sat down in their original places, contemplating their own grievances.

The atmosphere inside the classroom began to sour as everyone started to remember their sources of unhappiness; some even began to cry. What were we to do, what would happen to us? How were we to be Rebaked, and for how long—would we be paid our usual salaries during our years back in the alma mater, would they count toward the total service we needed to complete for our pensions? The room quickly collapsed into anarchy. At this moment, our old lifestyle representative, Hu Pingping, stood up and walked quickly, if nervously, up to the podium. "I'd like to say a few words about my own thoughts and feelings," she faltered, glancing around the room with teary eyes. "I won't go into the details of what I've gone through over the past decade. I've had job troubles, I've been divorced. My health has gone downhill. You can probably tell just by looking at me. At times, I lost all hope: I've thought about dying. In fact, I've tried to kill myself. But here we all are now. Surely this is a sign things have taken a turn for the better. This is destiny, I'm sure. We all can make new beginnings. Isn't a fresh start the most beautiful, wonderful thing in the world? We're all adults now. We should all be able to cope with this challenge, to move forward. After all, the individual is nothing. Our lives have meaning only when we merge with society."

Applause rippled faintly through the classroom. I felt a chill run up my spine. Though Hu Pingping seemed to have plenty more to say for herself, fortunately at this moment the tutor rushed back in. "The bus is here," he shouted, waving his arms to get us moving. "Everyone on board!" A brand-new luxury coach had pulled up outside the building. We were being dispatched outside the city, to a distant extension of the campus, because the university itself was too full to accommodate us. The new campus was apparently at the foot of a mountain somewhere: though it was in the middle of nowhere, there were lakes and rivers all around, and the scenery was supposed to be beautiful. The compound itself had been commissioned especially for Operation Rebake. The tutor stood by the coach, ticking off names, one by one, from the register; no one could get on until they'd been crossed off. That way no one would manage to slip the net. As I had been the last to register, I was the last on the bus. When I got on, I discovered the only free seat was next to Hu Pingping. I gritted my teeth and sat down. Darkness had completely fallen before we were even out of the main gates. I could sense Hu Pingping's restlessness; I knew that she was feeling frustrated at not having been allowed to finish her Henry V speech. Closing my eyes, I leaned back against the seat, determined not to say a single word to her.

I'd hoped we'd reach our destination quickly, but two hours later we were still driving. The more impatient of our number started asking the driver how much farther it was: they were starving, they said. The driver just drove, without acknowledging any of the questions. He didn't even turn around; throughout the journey, we saw him only from the back—his bull's neck was even wider than his head. The bus gradually fell silent; everyone's blood sugar was too low to chat any more. I cradled my grumbling stomach with my hands and hoped I might fall asleep. But Hu Pingping suddenly whispered something in my ear: "I hope we're riding to our deaths." Needless to say, I didn't much feel like sleeping after that. I looked anxiously around me. Outside, it was pitch-dark; I had no idea where we were. "Why d'you say something like that?" I asked her uneasily. "Just making conversation," she replied. "And at least that way, we could die together. Even though we're sitting next to each other on this bus, I feel like you're a universe away from me." Realizing it was just another Hu Pingping fantasy, I relaxed. "Don't make me sick. Look, for the last time: I don't love you. In fact, I hate you." "That doesn't matter," she replied. "I'm sure we'll come back together in the next life. Next time, everything will be better." "Cut that out," I interrupted. "Forget it." Hu Pingping now raised her voice: "Why?" I began shouting too: "Why? You lied to me ten years ago, and you're still lying to me now. What hope is there for us?" Hu Pingping began to cry, oblivious to everyone around her. After a while, she wiped her eyes with her sleeve and stood up. "Why won't you believe me?" she bellowed, as if we were hundreds of miles apart, at opposite ends of a wilderness. "I swear I wasn't lying. I'm sick and tired of telling you. You know your problem? You've never loved anyone because there's no love in you. And that's why you can never believe in anything!"

Another smattering of applause rippled through the bus; out of the darkness, someone started to whistle. I let out one more expletive in my head, then leaned back and closed my eyes.

DA MA'S **WAY OF TALKIN**
THE **MATCHMAKER**
THE **APPRENTICE**
THE **FOOTBALL FA**
XIAO **LIU**
MR. HU, ARE YOU COMI
REEDUCATIO

THE **WHARF**

Gongbu—the southeastern kingdom that the Buddhist master Padmasambhava called the Capital of the Dead—refuses to celebrate New Year on the same day that the rest of Tibet does. In Gongbu, it falls on the first day of the tenth month of the Tibetan calendar, for reasons that drift back seven hundred years, to the reign of King Ajiejiebu. The people of Gongbu say—they've always said—that although King Niechi gave them their independence, it's the heroic Ajiejiebu they should thank for their courage. One year, as deep autumn turned into winter, Ajiejiebu called together every fighting man to meet an invading army that had broken through the region's northern rim. But thoughts of the fat pork and barley wine of New Year had driven all the fighting spirit out of Gongbu's braves. So Ajiejiebu decided to shift the New Year to the first day of the tenth month. Their celebrations completed, the merry men of Gongbu marched off fearlessly to rout their enemy in battle. But it was in the last campaign of the war, legend goes, that Ajiejiebu was killed and his head and limbs were hacked from his body. As they marched home, the sons of Gongbu carried aloft the dismembered torso of their leader, their songs of victory saddened by funeral bugles.

Even though the Gongbu New Year was still three weeks away, Gesang wanted to be home, back in Changdu, where his wife and the newborn son he'd never seen were waiting for him. He'd tried asking for leave, but his travel company—a Lhasa-based outfit that managed the boat trips up and down the Tsampo River—wouldn't let him go. Around twenty years old and new to the job, Gesang was the sole caretaker at the wharf that served Pai, the final stop for tourists along the Tsampo River and the jumping-off point for visitors to Tsampo Gorge. By the last month or two of the lunar year, tourists were pretty scarce, but still Gesang had to keep an eye on things. If he left, there would be no one else to look after the place. He understood this, and it was worrying him.

After breakfast, four aging backpackers who'd arrived the evening before picked up their bags, said good-bye to Gesang, and set off toward Motuo. The wharf fell quiet again. Gesang carried outside the pot of noodles the travelers had only half finished, slopped the leftovers into a trough, then made a loud gurgling call. The pig showed no interest in appearing.

"Little bastard." Gesang's face wrinkled with anxiety.

Something else occurred to him. Still carrying the dripping bowl, he headed for the guest rooms. The inner flank of the building—behind the waiting room that overlooked the river—was divided into three dormitories laid out with beds for travelers who had missed their crossing; the last of these had, for the time being, been taken over by Gesang. With far more violence than was necessary, he shoved open the door to the middle room, the wood banging against the wall. Only one of the room's four beds was taken—the one farthest from the door. Its motionless occupant, curled up into a ball under his quilt, his coat spread over the top, faced the wall. Gesang briskly, noisily remade the bed nearest the doorway; still his guest failed to move.

"Are you leaving today?" Gesang asked.

"No," the man replied, his left hand emerging to tug the coat over his head.

"When, then?"

"That's my business."

"It's mine, too!" Gesang almost shouted.

There was no response.

"Would you mind telling me where you're headed?" Gesang tried a slightly milder approach.

Still no answer. Eventually, Gesang stormed off, leaving the door open. He shouldn't have let the man stay. Not that it had really been up to him. Ten days ago, the visitor had stepped off the boat along with a tour group of old Chinese cadres and failed to move on. He'd brought nothing with him except an expensive-looking leather briefcase that he carried over his shoulder. His face had a sick, sad pallor to it. Though Gesang found it hard to age Chinese people, he put this one around forty. He seemed to know his way around the wharf, though; he had made straight for the dormitories. Even then, there was something about him that had made Gesang faintly uneasy.

"Why don't you stay in Pai?" Gesang had blurted out. He had a point, though. The wharf was quite a distance from the town it served; it was too isolated, too desolate, especially at night, while Pai—set within the region of Nyingchi—had become much more tourist friendly in recent years. Most visitors either went back to Bayi or on to Pai. The Chinese man glanced expressionlessly back at Gesang, who now wondered what the hell he was trying to do, driving business away.

"It's forty *yuan* a night—payment in advance."

After a slight hesitation, the man drew a wad of notes from his pocket, handed four of them to Gesang and then turned away again. Examining them, Gesang saw that they were each a hundred *yuan*.

"How long are you planning to stay?" he asked, now bewildered.

"Don't know." The man didn't even look back.

*

The wharf was screened, almost secretively, by three stout, ancient trees, each of whose trunks it would have taken four or five arm spans to encircle. The wharf's back wall seemed to merge into the cliffs that rose up behind it, and had it not been for the landing stages, approaching passengers might have missed it altogether, mistaking it for a stone cave perched amid the branches. The quay became conspicuous only when tourist boats—stridently announced by their steam whistles—came into the dock. Once onshore, visitors followed a roughly paved road up from the river until at last the building emerged before them: the waiting room to the right, an underused dining room to the left, the two rooms divided by a stone ramp that led up to a view of the mountains behind. Once you finally had it in your sights, it looked out of place, out of time, perhaps due to its size or design—as if it really shouldn't have been there. It seemed wrong for a wilderness—it looked more like a dacha, a country getaway. Any life to the place was only temporary. Once the travelers had scattered and the boats cast off, the wharf would disappear back into stillness.

Since his arrival—apart from an initial foray into Pai to buy food and drink—the Chinese man had spent every day inside at the wharf. Gesang couldn't understand why he slept so much during the day: what kind of tourist never went out? Whenever a boat steamed up, he would retreat to his own room and shut the door. He seemed to be waiting for someone, or perhaps not. Apart from the occasional Tibetan from one of the handful of villages that lined the Tsampo Gorge, most of the passengers were tourists. And for three days, no boat had come. Since it had rained during the nights, the days should have been crisply bright. Instead, they had dawned chillingly overcast, with the sun struggling hazily into view only at around ten in the morning.

Perhaps drawn out by this weak sunshine, the man clambered up the stone ramp to the railed rooftop terrace that looked out over the river from the roof of the wharf, his thinness and pallor underscored by the daylight. He panted for oxygen through his brief excursion, looking anxiously about him as he walked. By the time he reached the deserted terrace, a thick blanket of cloud had grayed the sky again. He staggered at a sudden gust of wind off the river; a mass of shriveled yellow leaves scattered off the tree that clung to the roof. Leaning forward, he reached out for the low iron railings to steady himself, but the frozen metal quickly forced him to let go. Although it was early winter, the thickly forested mountains on both sides of the river were still sharp with green; the water was murky by comparison.

He watched the river course eastward. About two miles away, Tsampo Gorge stared straight back at him, as if he could reach out and touch it. Just before the river swelled out into a vast lake was a strange, solitary little island squatting in the center of the narrow mouth to the gorge: Demon Island—locals called it the Castle of Luosha, one of the great demons of Indian mythology. When Padmasambhava first reached these parts, he had defeated the local demons led by the king of Gongbu only by winning over the kingdom's guardian spirit, Gongzundemu, whom he ordered to hold this island as a fastness against evil. The faint outlines of a building were just visible, a small temple to the spirit. Farther on lay Namcha Barwa, the easternmost anchor of the Himalayas, its pinnacle obscured by the wreath of cloud that hung around it all year long. As if disappointed to be denied a clear sighting, the man closed his eyes.

A line of white prayer flags rose up from the gorge's steep right-hand bank, marking—as legend told it—the nine turrets of the royal castle of Gongbu. The Chinese man stared out over the stone ruins, his clothes fluttering like the prayer flags in the wind.

> My lover headed
> Towards the prayer flags
> On the mountains of Beila
> May the wind carry my prayers there, too.

A gurgling call interrupted his thoughts: it was Gesang, charging along the dirt road up to town. Frozen, bewildered, the man set off back down the ramp, his coat wrapped tightly around him. Gesang didn't even notice him—he had thoughts only for his pig.

*

The Zangxiang pig—with its sharp trotters and spindly tail—is a breed indigenous only to Tibet. They're mostly reared free-range, allowed to wander all over the mountains, their flesh sweetened by the spring water they drink and the soft, fine carpets of caterpillar fungus they nibble. A great favorite with tourists, their price had rocketed over the past few years. Since a full-grown specimen would fetch three thousand or four thousand *yuan* and even a piglet could go for four hundred, raising them had swiftly become the locals' second most profitable sideline, after illegal logging. Gesang's first idea had been to keep a mastiff for company in the deserted wharf. But there was no money to be made out of a mastiff. So he settled on a pig instead, for social and financial reasons. Because his salary was modest, he decided to start off with just one and see how much money he could make out of it when it grew to full size. That was the plan.

His first pig swiftly disappeared into someone else's herd. The loss sharpened him up: why, he berated himself, hadn't he left a mark on it? The moment he got back with pig number 2, he gave it a full coat of Propaganda Red—the angry scarlet paint the party used for sloganeering around the countryside. He rejoiced in the knowledge that his was the reddest pig in Tibet: it could run away to China and he'd still be able to pick it out. Ten days later, the animal was shot dead on the hills by a local hunter, who'd mistaken it for something else—he'd never seen a pig like it in his forty years. For a brief while, though, a happy ending seemed in sight. The huntsman kept six pigs—even the smallest of which was much fatter than Gesang's—and offered one as compensation. But before Gesang could congratulate himself on his unexpected good fortune, the hunter produced a wooden truncheon, broke the pig's front leg and handed it over. Too embarrassed to object, Gesang carried the animal, squealing with agony, back home. For days, Gesang hardly slept, as the pig's cries of grief echoed over the river. Thanks to Gesang's ministrations, the leg mended almost perfectly. But then something new began to trouble Gesang: the pig's left buttock still bore the brand of its original owner. How could he prove it was his, and not someone else's? The problem cost him another sleepless night. Early the next day, a solution finally came to him. While the pig was at the trough, snuffling through some barley mush, he snipped off its inconsequential tail with a pair of scissors. Crazy with pain, the pig danced up and down the quayside, trailing blood behind it. Still holding the scissors, Gesang stared curiously down at the tail on the ground, kicking it back and forth. At last, Gesang told himself, the world will know that mine is the pig without a tail. As this thought occurred to him, the traumatized, tail-less pig galloped up the slope to the terrace, took off through the railings, and fell to its death on the paving stones below. When Gesang rushed over, the rims of its eyes—fixed gently ahead—were sputtering blood. His was indeed the pig without a tail, but not for long.

The whole business affected Gesang badly. After six pig-free months, though, a chance encounter with a piebald piglet at a farmers' market brought about a change of heart. The animal had not only the same gentle eyes as the second pig but also the same lack of tail. It had been born like that, its owner told him. Gesang knew instantly that this was the reincarnation of his last pig. It was destiny; he had to have it. But as something still tugged him back from a decision, his mobile rang—it was his wife, telling him she'd had a baby boy. His eyes hot with tears, Gesang scooped up the pig and hurried off home with it.

And it was this reincarnation that Gesang was now searching for. Back and forth he walked along the dirt road to town, shouting himself hoarse, asking everyone he met: "Seen a pig without a tail?"

Gesang couldn't understand why so many people laughed. By evening, Gesang gave up all hope and despondently headed home. But just before a roadside cairn, he pulled up disbelievingly. A pig was spread-eagled, flat as a flayed pelt, over the soft, wet road. Faint wheel marks over its spine betrayed the work of a lumbering timber truck. In death, as in life, the pig's blank eyes stared gently ahead. His knees weakening, Gesang sank to the ground, scrabbling to unearth the pig's bloody, fleshy buttocks. It had no tail.

He could not understand why pig keeping was so hard for him and so easy for others; why life was so unfair. Fury clutched at his young Gongbu heart. His next piglet, he vowed, would live. But for now, his capital had run out.

✶

A faintly hysterical Gesang rushed back to the wharf, searching everywhere for the Chinese man, as if he were the murderer of his beloved pig. He had to blame someone—anyone, and the Chinese man was the only available scapegoat. Gesang furiously kicked open the door to the guest room. The briefcase was lying on the bed, its owner nowhere to be seen. Gesang swung the bag against the wall, listening hopefully for the sound of something breaking inside. Quickly bored with punishing inanimate objects, he threw down the bag and rushed back out. Since he didn't know the man's name, he just ran up and down the quayside, hollering. Luckily, the man failed to appear, and after a few laps Gesang began to tire, to calm down. It was nothing to do with the Chinese man. Gesang now imagined how the last but one pig must have felt, when its tail had just been snipped off. He was suddenly jolted by the conviction that his pig was somehow still alive.

But as soon as Gesang saw the man again that evening, he felt his anger return. The visitor was sitting in the dining room, tending the fire, staring out of the window at the Tsampo River at dusk. The whole thing seemed completely unreal to Gesang. An exhausting mass of doubts and suspicions gnawed at him. How had the Chinese man got in here? The room hadn't been unlocked for ages. The fireplace had never been used since the wharf opened—it was usually piled with random junk. Gesang had barely even noticed it; how had the Chinese man known it was there? Where had he got the firewood from? Who'd said he could light a fire? Gesang wanted to do a great many things: to ask him all this, to shout at him, to throw him out of the window, to kick him into the river. Eventually, he compressed all his rage into a single accusation: "You owe me rent."

Which was not untrue. Ten days had passed; more money was due. The man—staring spellbound across the river at a mist of sand blowing over the bank—finally woke to Gesang's presence behind him. He turned slowly to look at Gesang, a little puzzled at the fury in his voice. To avoid meeting the man's eyes, Gesang gazed at the fireplace: it was a curious European design he'd never seen before. Slowly drawing from his pocket the wad of notes, the man handed over another four hundred. Although the pinewood fire was cracking and spitting with heat, his hands trembled violently. Gesang wanted, more than anything, to smash this quivering four hundred *yuan* back in his face. He didn't want his money, he wanted to tell him; he wanted him to get lost so Gesang could go home for New Year. But how could Gesang refuse another four hundred *yuan*? He could buy a piglet with that. After a brief hesitation, he snatched the money and pedantically counted the four notes.

"You were never here!" He suddenly glared at his visitor.

What did he mean? Don't tell anyone you were here, perhaps; I want to keep this money for myself. The man stared blankly back at him and then nodded mechanically, without asking for further clarification. As soon as he'd left the room, Gesang gave the base of the wall a violent kick. He hated himself for not having screamed at his Chinese visitor. And now he'd kicked the wall too hard; his heart ached with the pain in his right foot. Gesang limped off, remembering his pig. It was still alive; he knew it.

*

Zhaxi reached the wharf at five in the morning. After knocking on every door and window in the building, he eventually roused Gesang, who poked his head out of the door, half-asleep and wrapped in his quilt. Dawn was a little way off still, and the mist outside the door had not yet cleared. His visitor, he saw, was draped in a black wool gown, with a bone-handled dagger at the waist, leading a black horse. Gesang slammed the door so fast he almost trapped his hand. He must be dreaming still, about the ghost of the king of Gongbu coming for him, to punish him for what he'd done. "Don't take me away!" he sobbed.

Four words from his visitor dispelled the pall of the supernatural: "I've got the pig."

Embarrassed, Gesang quickly tugged on his clothes and opened the door, smiling as hard as he could. Gesang had first met Zhaxi—who lived in Zhibai, one of the nearby villages—when the old man had wanted to pair him up with his granddaughter, Zhuoma. She was very pretty and had a beautiful singing voice, but there was a small white cataract in her left eye that had made Gesang uneasy. See that cloud in the sky? the old man asked him. It's like having one of them in your eye. Gesang nodded, still unsure. Fortunately, he was already promised to someone in his own village, the woman who was now his wife; otherwise he would have drifted anxiously into it. Today, though, Zhaxi was here on other business. Gesang had asked him to find him another piglet; this time, he'd emphasized, he wanted a girl.

"Much easier to find a boy," Zhaxi had objected.

"It has to be a girl."

Gesang's pig-rearing failures had made him superstitious; perhaps trying the female of the species would change his luck. Zhaxi untied the piglet hanging upside down by its hind legs from his saddle and set it down next to Gesang. Tethered by a meter of rope, the piglet staggered woozily about, dazed by its bumpy journey. Gesang squatted down, patiently waiting for it to come around. Zhaxi lit his pipe, blowing a thick blanket of smoke over the animal's snout. To Gesang's partial relief, it snorted groggily. Zhaxi asked Gesang what his plans were: if he wasn't going home, he ought to spend New Year at Zhibai. But Gesang didn't want to risk it, as he'd heard that Zhuoma was still unmarried. He stroked the piglet's fine tail while he made his excuses. But as he reached, almost without thinking, between the piglet's hind legs, he suddenly whipped back his hand as if scalded. "It's a boy!" "Impossible," Zhaxi said, keeping on with his pipe. Gesang turned the pig on its back and splayed its hind legs in Zhaxi's direction. Now that dawn had broken, Zhaxi had a clear view. Almost dropping his pipe in surprise, he came over and rammed his nose in the pig's groin. "How the hell did that happen?" Zhaxi muttered to himself, vexed by the pig's sudden sex change, tugging the penis back and forth with his stubby index finger, as if wanting to pull the thing out.

"I won't take it." Gesang stood up, shaking his head. Scowling, Zhaxi said nothing. The two men faced each other.

Gesang gave the pig an impatient kick on the buttocks; no response. He gave it a second kick: a bit harder this time, a bit angrier. Male and barely alive, this pig—in Gesang's eyes—was highly defective. At this moment, something seemed to snap in Zhaxi. Whipping the dagger from his waist, he threw away the scabbard and yanked apart the piglet's legs apart.

"What the hell are—" Gesang screeched.

An instant later, the penis was gone. With a honk of pain, the piglet shot up out of its stupor and stared about in wild confusion. When it finally worked out what had happened, the poor animal tried to charge off, squealing with horror. Zhaxi quickly grabbed hold of the halter, hanging on while the piglet ran bloody circles around him. At this point, the black horse also took fright and stampeded. Though Zhaxi yelled at Gesang to stop it, the young man stood paralyzed with shock, both legs jammed together. Fortunately, the horse chose a dead end; when it came back in the opposite direction, Gesang could seize its reins. Horse and pig now ran laps around the two men.

"Happy now?" Zhaxi shouted at Gesang, as both struggled to restrain the animals.

"It's still not a girl!"

"I did you a favor, cutting that thing off!"

"Why don't you cut your own off, then?"

The horse calmed down first. Eventually, the black pig did too and lay on the ground as if stunned. The two men threw down their ropes and stood there, panting. There was an angry pallor to Zhaxi's face. Gesang didn't dare look up at him: he knew he shouldn't have said what he'd just said. He could only hope the old man hadn't heard him. Quiet returned to the wharf, disturbed only by the pig's groans.

A man approached, silent as a shadow. The Chinese man. Wherever he'd been, he looked exhausted. His lips were a ghostly white, his empty eyes framed by wildly disheveled hair. When he passed wordlessly between Gesang and Zhaxi, as if he hadn't even seen them, Gesang could feel his bone-piercing coldness. The man went in through the waiting room and disappeared into the darkness inside. Gesang stared vacantly after him.

"Poisoned," Zhaxi observed.

"What?"

Gesang glanced doubtfully at the old man. Zhaxi motioned inside with his chin. Gesang felt every hair on his head stand up, his spine skittering with shivers. He was starting to understand.

*

He liked the evenings here, so quiet you could hear your own heart beat. He could imagine he was almost floating along on the river, his body warming as if he were returning to the womb. When he woke in the night, he had given up trying to work out whether he was awake or dreaming. He had abandoned all consciousness of time, all need to wake at prescribed times—it was wonderful.

He sat up, pulled on his coat, then got up, and slowly pulled on his trousers and shoes. He hated shoes with laces and trousers with button flies. Every outline in the room was clear, as if it had been washed by moonlight. One step after another took him toward the door; but as soon as he had gone out, he hesitated: should he take his mobile phones? Go on then, a voice told him. One step after another took him back into the room. He groped around his bed until he found his bag. But there seemed to be something wrong with the phones when he found them. He tipped the bag's contents onto the bed. Both his phones were in pieces: screen, battery, cover. Though he tried to reassemble them, he couldn't quite do it because they were different makes. He started to sweat with anxiety; his fingers began to disobey him. Why couldn't he do something so simple? He was about to cry with the frustration of it.

Eventually, irritation woke him. He looked around him, then out of the window. He must have been dreaming, he thought. As soon as he saw the pile of mobile parts on the bed, he felt unsure again.

Going out a second time, he approached Gesang's room, pressed his ear to the door, and heard a regular snore. He gently pushed on the door; it was bolted from inside. He now plodded back to his own room and sat on the bed, fighting the desire to go to sleep. Something was making him uneasy.

The cold woke him the next time. He was now surrounded by crumbling, overgrown ruins. The darkness had slightly grayed; clouds hung thickly in the distance. Where was he? It was familiar, but also strange as if he were in a waking dream. Scrambling to his feet, he looked around. To his left a narrow flight of stone stairs led up to a bare, tamped-earth wall festooned with white prayer flags. He decided to climb up to see what lay beyond. With each step that he took, a great river extended before him. His eyes smarted with the familiarity of it—he sensed he was about to wake up. He accelerated until suddenly he almost stepped out into a void: when he looked down, he discovered he was standing on the edge of a precipice—one more step and he would have fallen to his death. He cried out with fear—he couldn't stop himself—but the sound was swallowed up by the canyon.

Now fully conscious, he recognized the ruins of the castle of the kings of Gongbu. His gaze swept the landscape before him, searching for the wharf. In the darkness before dawn, all he could see was the Tsampo rushing into the gorge; the wharf would be in that final bend of the river. He noticed that the black writing on the fluttering prayer flags had smudged. He closed his eyes, as if waiting for the wind to blow him off balance.

Black ink on white cloth,
Blurred after the rain.
However hard I try,
My feelings can never be unwritten.

By the time he got back to the wharf, day had properly broken. He could hardly believe he had walked so far. He was almost delirious with exhaustion, unsure whether he was dreaming or actually seeing the things he passed. Just as his craving for a bed had become almost unbearable, the wharf appeared before him, with a black horse and a black pig running circuits around two men. This—he had no doubt—was a hallucination.

★

How could he have been so careless, Gesang belabored himself: he'd almost let this Chinese man die in front of him. As he had no idea how much trouble the whole thing might bring to his door, the more he thought about it, the more afraid he became. Poisoning your enemies had a venerable pedigree in Gongbu. When he was small, Gesang had seen an old poison-woman dragged through the streets after she'd been caught, wooden stakes stuck into her fingers. Usually, you poisoned someone to steal their good luck: you stored the poison in your fingernails and then slipped it to your victim when he or she wasn't looking. Once the victim was dead, the theory went, all their blessings would pass to their murderer. Or sometimes, if a man was about to set off on a long journey, his lover would slip poison into his wine. If the man didn't come back when he said he would, he wouldn't get the antidote before the poison started to work. Though Gesang didn't know why the man had been poisoned, he was sure he would die soon. Gesang could only hope he'd hold on until his bosses arrived.

While the Chinese man slept, Gesang spent the day running between the terrace (to see whether any boats had come into view) and the man's room (to check whether he was still breathing). The castrated pig was in even worse shape than Gesang's visitor. Gesang had, in the end, bought it, for a hundred *yuan* less than the asking price, first because he was sorry he'd shouted at Zhaxi and second because he wanted to thank the old man for having pointed out the poisoning business to him. But he couldn't bring himself to feel any love for the animal. Gesang had found a filthy white *hada* scarf that a tourist had left behind and bound it clumsily around the piglet's groin to stop the bleeding. He'd then tried to find a suitable hiding place for the animal—he didn't want his bosses to know he was keeping a pig at the wharf. Finally, he tethered it to one corner of the terrace, figuring that they wouldn't go up there because it was too cold. Every time Gesang ran up to the terrace, the pig insisted on snorting at him. Even though Gesang's head was full of the Chinese man, he was still irritated by the fact that the piglet seemed to be deliberately trying to sound like a girl.

"Shut up or I'll poison *you*!"

Finally, at 3 P.M., the quiet of the Tsampo River was destroyed. Gesang had never seen anything like it in all his time at the wharf: a triangle of three speedboats trailing behind them six snowy trails of spray. His blood surged with the roaring of the motors. He jogged up to the river's edge and leaped onto the landing stage, waving as hard as he could.

About twenty grim-faced men disembarked. In addition to his travel company boss, the party included representatives from Public Security, Special Services, Public Hygiene, Tourist and Border Defense, as well as the local government. A Chinese man had been poisoned in Tibet: this was a serious business, especially after last year's riots. Gesang led the way, listening to the oppressive tread of task-force feet over the cobbles. His legs almost buckled at every step.

The man was lying motionless on the bed farthest away, facing the wall. When Gesang timidly stepped forward to remove the coat covering the man's head, he felt as if he were lifting a shroud. The corpse suddenly sat bolt up; everyone started with fright. Glancing around, the Chinese man discovered a dark, dense mass of people crowded around his bedside. A look of intense confusion overcame him, as if he were struggling to work out whether this was really happening. In the meantime, everyone else in the room inspected him back, trying to assess—from his own angle of expertise—the victim's situation. As the air inside the room seemed to congeal with the strangeness of it, a plaintive squeal drifted in from outside, a squeal that only Gesang could identify.

After this had gone on some time, an overweight man shoved his way up to the bed through the crowd. "Dr. Zhang!" He began pumping the Chinese man's hand. "What are you doing here? Did you come all the way from Beijing?" After a second, the Chinese man recognized his interlocutor. "Who . . . ?" He motioned around at everyone else in the room. "This is Dr. Zhang, the great architect!" the overweight man explained to everyone else rather overexcitedly. "He designed the wharf." No one seemed particularly cheered by this news. Not only had a Chinese man been poisoned; he was also one of the great architects of Tibetan development. It was all so much worse than they had first feared. Now it was the turn of a Public Security man with burning eyes to approach Dr. Zhang's bedside. "When," he wanted to know, "did you discover you'd been poisoned?" Bemusement flickered back onto the great architect's face. "Poisoned?" he mumbled, frowning. "I just wanted to come back here—I've wanted to for years. But there never seemed to be time. Until now. So I just decided to come—I didn't want to put you to any trouble, that's why I didn't tell anyone. What's all this about poison?" Every gaze now swept onto Gesang. The suddenness of it paralyzed him, as if he had been nailed to the ground. A second plaintive squeal floated into the room, a squeal that, once more, only Gesang could identify.

✶

As far as Gesang was concerned, everything that happened next was a nightmare. Each dignitary personally, individually took responsibility for swearing at him. Because each of them was so very eminent and was from a different department, no one wanted simply to replicate any of the lectures that had already been delivered—that would have been far too facile, too unimaginative. So they pushed their creativity to its limits, searching for inventive new ways to humiliate him. Eventually, Gesang burst into tears, not because of all the shouting, but because so much of it was incomprehensible to him. "He's Tibetan," someone finally whispered, "best lay off." The special task force withdrew, their suits rustling.

Only the corpulent director of the travel agency remained, instructed by *his* bosses to look after the architect. Dr. Zhang realized he couldn't stay here any longer and decided to go back to Beijing the next day. The director was full of suggestions for the architect's last night, but every one of them was refused: he just wanted to stay at the wharf he had designed. Like a good host, the director had to humor his guest and contented himself by organizing a farewell banquet. His savaging at an end, Gesang now spent the rest of the day fetching and carrying between Pai and the wharf. He couldn't understand why he, who wanted to go home, couldn't, while the Chinese man, who didn't want to go home, could. After all the trouble his visitor had caused him, Gesang now had to go and get him barley wine. The very thought of it made Gesang want to poison it, not to kill him, just to give his stomach a good turn. As night set in, the director, along with a few government officials from Pai, began raucously fêting the architect in the dining room.

While Gesang was struggling to work out how to keep the fire going—it was different from the charcoal braziers he was used to—his boss (who had drunk himself into a good mood) suddenly called him over to drink a toast as a penalty. "He," he slurred to the architect, pointing at Gesang, "was the one who said you'd been poisoned." He *had* been poisoned, the architect spoke up for Gesang. So was everyone who came to this part of the country: they either couldn't leave or were always wanting to come back. What a way with words Dr. Zhang had, everyone agreed.

Holding aloft a bowl of barley wine, Gesang's face was flushed with discomfort. Hoping to put Gesang at his ease, the architect got up to clink bowls with him. "I was never here," he said, with a wink. Gesang's head went blank with shock—he didn't realize it was a joke. What would happen to him if all these men from the government found out what he'd done? As Gesang was about to gulp the wine down, his boss stopped him. "Don't be such a savage. Come on, sing us a drinking song first!" Gesang's head remained blank. "I don't know any," he mumbled. The director refused to believe him: A Tibetan not know any drinking songs? Impossible! Sing! When Gesang insisted that he really didn't know one, the director started swearing at him again, this time drunkenly. "Forget it," the architect cut in. Still the director wouldn't give up. "Just sing anything, any Tibetan hunting song. How about 'Good Luck' or 'On the Golden Mountain in Beijing'? You must know 'The Golden Mountain.'" Realizing he didn't have a choice, Gesang sang it through in Tibetan. He felt he sang badly—as if someone had him by the throat as he croaked his way through it—but his audience applauded him enthusiastically. At last, the architect and Gesang could drink their wine while the fat director recovered his good spirits and rewarded Gesang with a hunk of yak meat and a bear hug. "Not a patch on Zhuoma, of course," he said. "But she's a girl," Gesang shyly objected. "I can't sing high the way she can." "What are you talking about?" his boss argued back, staring hard at him. "Bet you'd sing higher than her if I chopped your balls off." The whole room roared with laughter. Gesang's Chinese wasn't quite good enough to catch what the director said, but he joined in anyway.

*

The architect tossed and turned, thinking of his journey back tomorrow. His reassembled mobile phones lay by his pillow. After a final hesitation, he turned them back on. In seconds, they began generating messages.

He thought back to the day that he had left Beijing. Because of a project in Shenzhen, he'd practically been living at the office for the best part of a week and had fallen asleep, exhausted, on the sofa. At five that morning, he had sat up, suddenly convinced he was about to miss a plane. Picking up his briefcase, he staggered out of the door and grabbed a taxi to take him to the airport, urging the driver to hurry. Finally, in the empty departure lounge, he woke up from his dream. He was seized by depression, not because of the sleepwalking—that had happened to him before—but because he realized he would have to go back to work. After a cup of coffee in the Starbucks at the airport, he had an idea: why not carry on with the dream? As if he'd never woken up. He took out both mobile phones and turned them off.

Two hours later, he lay on his bed, all the phone calls he needed to make out of the way; at last he felt sleepy. He thought vaguely of tomorrow, about the director coming over first thing, along with some vice president from somewhere else. There would be no more opportunity to explore, to say good-bye to the gorge. Regret prickled him. Then he fell asleep.

It was a full moon. The still air felt moister than it did during the day, as if touched by the warmth of a spring night. He climbed slowly up the ramp, looking anxiously about as he walked. At last, he stood to one side of the terrace. The Tsampo River hung in the air before him like a great, long snake of silver-white silk. By night, it seemed to have a soft suppleness that it lacked during the days.

He stood there, staring out into the canyon. He shut his oxygen-starved eyes, taking greedy gulps of air, thinking about the river coursing into the canyon—a long antenna exploring the world's last perfect wilderness, hemmed in by the gorge. A curious, long lost sense of excitement seized hold of him and his hand slipped inside his trousers.

Waves of pleasure, mimicking the pull of the river, rippled through him as his breathing grew labored, his body hotter. At the point of ejaculation, Namcha Barwa suddenly emerged from deep within the gorge, pulling clear of the clouds that usually surrounded its summit—he was sure of it. For the briefest of instants, the happiness was too much for him. He lay down.

✶

Despite the short notice, the director had prepared vast numbers of local specialties for the architect to take back with him to Beijing. Bag after bag of them Gesang had had to drag onto the motorboat. But he didn't mind because he thought once he'd got rid of his unwanted visitors, he could go home. Last to embark was his boss, whom Gesang carefully helped on board. This was his last chance, he thought.

"Would it be all right, sir, if I went home now?"

But the director suddenly remembered a piece of turquoise sent by the mayor that he'd left in the waiting room. Gesang ran back to get it. He couldn't believe his eyes: it was an enormous, uncut slab of stone weighing at least 110 pounds. By the time Gesang had hauled it over to the boat, he was too out of breath to say or do anything, except stand on the landing stage, watching the boat swagger off upriver.

When he had recovered, Gesang thought it was time to go and deal with the pig. He'd changed his mind: he'd decided to slaughter it. Pigs were there to be killed and eaten as well as reared. There was still some barley wine leftover from yesterday. Thinking he'd celebrate New Year early, he began to cheer up.

But only an empty tether and a wind-dried bloodstain remained where he'd tied it yesterday. His transsexual pig had disappeared. This time, Gesang didn't bother looking for him. He squatted down on the terrace and realized he wasn't cut out for this life. Why should he run around after other people all the time? Why couldn't he go home to spend New Year's with his wife and son? So he left. He never came back.

✶

The pig was cold and hungry and had lost a dangerous amount of blood. Around midnight, as it was nearing death, someone or something trod on its thin tail; though its impulse was to recoil, it was too weak to move. A little later, a few drops of hot liquid fell into its open mouth. Gulping them down, it managed to struggle to its feet, licked the rest of the warm stuff from the ground, and then lay down again. At four or five in the morning, the pig stood up as if in a dream and easily—the noose had grown too big for its undernourished neck—slipped out of its tether. On trembling legs, it walked down the ramp from the terrace and along the side of the wharf, resting every few paces against the wall as if checking it was going the right way. Halfway down the stone path to the riverside, it gave up and rolled a while, then stood up and crawled on until it could move no more, and a rush of warmth suddenly bore it aloft.

As if dead to the world, it bobbed along in the river until eventually its head collided with a rock. The pig now woke, unable to understand what it was doing in the water. As it did not, of course, want to drown, it began struggling toward a bank. Once on dry land, it shook the drops of water off its body and looked around. It had no idea where it was.

Two or three hours later, when the sun rose, the pig finally understood that it had become the sole resident of Demon Island.

After a long, hard winter, during which the pig somehow survived by eating everything that could be eaten on the island, it was discovered by a devout local come to burn incense for Gongbu's guardian spirit, who acclaimed it a Holy Pig. From this point on, it grew to be the happiest, fattest pig in Tibet, feasting on offerings, worshipped by multitudes. Its clumsily foreshortened penis only heightened its cult.

The Holy Pig of Demon Island drew waves of curious tourists until this once-quiet wharf developed into a bustling port. When the sun was out, the pig would stand on its island, looking out magisterially, watching the Tsampo River roll toward it, convinced that it was its guardian spirit.

And so it was that the world's last perfect wilderness was destroyed by a pig.

WEATHERHEAD BOOKS ON ASIA

Weatherhead East Asian Institute, Columbia University

LITERATURE

DAVID DER-WEI WANG, EDITOR

Ye Zhaoyan	*Nanjing 1937: A Love Story*, translated by Michael Berry (2003)
Oda Makato	*The Breaking Jewel*, translated by Donald Keene (2003)
Han Shaogong	*A Dictionary of Maqiao*, translated by Julia Lovell (2003)
Takahashi Takako	*Lonely Woman*, translated by Maryellen Toman Mori (2004)
Chen Ran	*A Private Life*, translated by John Howard-Gibbon (2004)
Eileen Chang	*Written on Water*, translated by Andrew F. Jones (2004)
Amy D. Dooling, Ed.	*Writing Women in Modern China: The Revolutionary Years, 1936–1976* (2005)
Han Bangqing	*The Sing-song Girls of Shanghai*, first translated by Eileen Chang, revised and edited by Eva Hung (2005)
Aili Mu, Julie Chiu, and Howard Goldblatt, Eds.	*Loud Sparrows: Contemporary Chinese Short-Shorts* (2006)
Hiratsuka Raichō	*In the Beginning, Woman Was the Sun*, translated by Teruko Craig (2006)
Zhu Wen	*I Love Dollars and Other Stories of China*, translated by Julia Lovell (2007)
Kim Sowŏl	*Azaleas: A Book of Poems*, translated by David McCann (2007)
Wang Anyi	*The Song of Everlasting Sorrow: A Novel of Shanghai*, translated by Michael Berry with Susan Chan Egan (2008)
Ch'oe Yun	*There a Petal Silently Falls: Three Stories by Ch'oe Yun*, translated by Bruce and Ju-Chan Fulton (2008)
Inoue Yasushi	*The Blue Wolf: A Novel of the Life of Chinggis Khan*, translated by Joshua A. Fogel (2009)
Anonymous	*Courtesans and Opium: Romantic Illusions of the Fool of Yangzhou*, translated by Patrick Hanan (2009)
Cao Naiqian	*There's Nothing I Can Do When I Think of You Late at Night*, translated by John Balcom (2009)
Park Wan-suh	*Who Ate Up All the Shinga? An Autobiographical Novel*, translated by Yu Young-nan and Stephen J. Epstein (2009)
Yi T'aejun	*Eastern Sentiments*, translated by Janet Poole (2009)
Hwang Sunwŏn	*Lost Souls: Stories*, translated by Bruce and Ju-Chan Fulton (2009)
Kim Sŏk-pŏm	*The Curious Tale of Mandogi's Ghost*, translated by Cindy Textor (2010)
Xiaomei Chen, Ed.	*The Columbia Anthology of Modern Chinese Drama* (2011)

Qian Zhongshu	*Humans, Beasts, and Ghosts: Stories and Essays*, edited by Christopher G. Rea, translated by Dennis T. Hu, Nathan K. Mao, Yiran Mao, Christopher G. Rea, and Philip F. Williams (2011)
Dung Kai-cheung	*Atlas: The Archaeology of an Imaginary City*, translated by Dung Kai-cheung, Anders Hansson, and Bonnie S. McDougall (2012)
O Chŏnghŭi	*River of Fire and Other Stories*, translated by Bruce Fulton and Ju-Chan Fulton (2012)
Endō Shūsaku	*Kiku's Prayer: A Novel*, translated by Van Gessel (2013)
Li Rui	*Trees Without Wind: A Novel*, translated by John Balcom (2013)
Abe Kōbō	*The Border Within: Selected Writings of Abe Kōbō*, translated by Richard Calichman

HISTORY, SOCIETY, AND CULTURE

CAROL GLUCK, EDITOR

Takeuchi Yoshimi	*What Is Modernity? Writings of Takeuchi Yoshimi*, edited and translated, with an introduction, by Richard F. Calichman (2005)
Richard F. Calichman, Ed.	*Contemporary Japanese Thought*, translated. (2005)
Richard F. Calichman, Ed.	*Overcoming Modernity*, translated. (2008)
Natsume Sōseki	Theory of Literature *and Other Critical Writings*, edited and translated by Michael Bourdaghs, Atsuko Ueda, and Joseph A. Murphy (2009)
Kojin Karatani	*History and Repetition*, edited by Seiji M. Lippit (2012)